HOLIDAY

ANTHOLOGY

2010

TALES & TAILS

This book is a collection of original works, recipes and previously authored quotes related to December-holiday events, family favorites and animals.

Wishbone Publishing

Phoenix, Arizona

Published in the United States of America through:

Wishbone Publishing
Phoenix, Arizona

ISBN 0982996713
EAN 978-0982996713

*This anthology
is dedicated
to pet lovers
everywhere.*

TABLE OF CONTENTS

HOLIDAY ANTHOLOGY 2010

TALES & TAILS

GREEN PIECES

Biography: Drew Aquilina grew up in New Milford, Connecticut. His early interest and first thoughts about cartoons and cartooning were, of course, fueled by watching *The Wonderful World of Disney*. He drew his first cartoon when he was a student at Delaware Valley College in Pennsylvania where he shared a dorm room with a turtle named Iggman, or Iggy, and three lizards. The pets were a source of inspiration for stories and a year later, a full-fledged cartoonist was born. Aquilina's first cartoon strip originated as *Iggman on Campus* in 1987 after he transferred to the University of Massachusetts Amherst. That strip was published for three semesters in *The Collegian*, the UMass student paper. After graduating, the strip *Green Pieces©* was born and the strip was copyrighted and ran as a daily and weekly feature in three Connecticut newspapers. Aquilina attended Arizona State University in Tempe, Arizona, as an art student and the strip was published in the school paper.

As a professional cartoonist, Drew continues to produce a daily *Green Pieces©* strip and he awaits the publication of his first cartoon compilation, *Green Pieces: Green From the Pond Up*, in January 2011. He lives in Paradise Valley, Arizona, with his wife, Lisa, and their own version of *Green Pieces:* two dogs, a cat, numerous rabbits, squirrels, roadrunners, quail coveys, hummingbirds, love birds and cactus wrens.

> "The purity of a person's heart can be quickly measured by how they regard animals." ~ Anonymous

A TRUE STORY:
WHAT MOTHERS DO

By Bill Butler

A s a five year old, I didn't know that World War II was winding down. It was the second Christmas that my father would not be home. My mother, in her twenties then, worked all afternoon making tree decorations. The kitchen table was crowded with stars, globes and animals made of shiny paper. There was at least a dozen feet of chain made of colored paper hoops.

She explained that we would get a Christmas tree later in the evening. That's when the prices for them usually dropped. Just after sunset we bundled up against the chilly Manhattan night and walked the four blocks to a parking lot where they sold Christmas trees.

"How much is your cheapest tree?" my mother asked the man standing at the lot entrance.

He held his gloved hand over the fire in a steel barrel. His brown skin glowed in the flickering. "Two dollars Miss."

Her smile disappeared. "Nothing for less?" Minimum wage then was thirty-three cents an hour.

The man picked up a small tree branch and dropped it into the fire. "I just work here Miss, I can't change the price."

The sudden melancholy in my mother's face made me sad.

The man looked down at me for what felt like a long time, it probably was only moments. He pointed at a mound of branches, the size of a car, in the corner of the lot. "See that pile of cuttings? Behind it is a tree that we can't sell. You can have it for free."

"Thank you," my mother said. She nudged my shoulder.

"Thank you sir," I said.

We hurried to the back of the mound. There it was, a scrawny thing just a little taller than me leaning against the wire fence. It had a few branches, but was almost a ghost of a tree.

My mother shouted to the man, "Can we take some of these branches also?"

He waved his arm. "Take it all if you want to, Miss."

I hauled the tree and she carried a bundle of branches. We set the tree in the corner of the living room, away from the radiator. I couldn't imagine how we could hang many decorations on a tree that had only a few sparse branches.

She was smiling again. "Go to sleep now. Santa will decorate the tree for us."

I woke at dawn and rushed into the living room. To my amazement the tree had filled out. I couldn't even see the trunk anymore. And it had a beautiful natural shape. The decorations glistened in the morning light. The chain of blue, red, white and green paper draped gracefully around the tree. I almost didn't notice the presents wrapped in shiny paper under the tree.

Days later, curiosity made me examine the tree closely. Christmas evening, my mother had used wire from clothes hangers to somehow affix discarded branches to the almost nude tree trunk. She had carefully trimmed it with scissors to get its perfect shape.

A few days later my father returned from overseas. When I told him about the tree, something happened that I didn't understand at the time. Tears filled the eyes of that burley soldier.

Since then, I have seen many wonderful holidays. That Christmas remains as my favorite.

Biography: Bill Butler was born in New York City but didn't leave Manhattan until he was a teenager. Since then he served in the U.S. Army, was a private detective, a social worker and later became a Vocational Rehabilitation Counselor. He has been writing for about four years and authored a guide to assist those who recently acquired a spinal cord injury. He has completed one manuscript loosely based on what he learned while working as a private detective. He is currently working on a second manuscript.

> "Our task must be to free ourselves…by widening our circle of compassion to embrace all living creatures and the whole of nature and its beauty." ~ Albert Einstein

> "The greatness of a nation and its moral progress can be judged by the way its animals are treated." ~ Mahatma Gandhi

> "Animals are reliable, many full of love, true in their affections, predictable in their actions, grateful and loyal. Difficult standards for people to live up to." ~ Alfred A. Montapert

> "Any glimpse into the life of an animal quickens our own and makes it so much the larger and better in every way." ~ John Muir

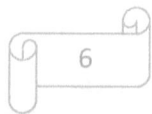

A FOREVER HOME

By Penni Ferry

I tried so hard to be good. I wanted to behave exactly like they wanted me to behave. I kept to myself in my own little world which was usually away from all of the others. Sometimes even that was not enough and I would be punished with a swat or two or angrily told to "shut up." I often wondered if I mattered to anyone.

Every night I would crawl into bed with my favorite blanket and say a special prayer that tomorrow would surely be a better day. I would often wish to be in a different place with a different life. Sometimes it was difficult to fall asleep so I would squint my eyes real tight and then think of beautiful things. I would slowly relax my eyes and that would calm me enough to drift away into my own world of slumber.

One night I had a dream that I had run away to find a better place to live. During this make believe time I had floated into an open field with lush greenery and flowers surrounded by huge pine trees. The fresh smell of the pine was such a pleasant change at first. Then as I looked down on myself in the field, I realized I was there all alone. I became scared. My heart started to race and breathing became difficult. I squinted and relaxed my eyes. When I got the nerve to open my eyes, I looked all around me and saw it was still dark outside. It still took me quite a while longer to realize it was just a dream. I finally accepted that I was safe and secure in my own bed with my favorite blanket and I felt better. I was so grateful that I had a roof over my head and a bed and blanket to call my own. It reminded me to be careful of what I would wish for.

Then about three weeks later in the middle of the night, I thought I was having another dream. It felt like I was floating in air again. I felt around me to make sure that I was still in my bed with my favorite blanket like I was when I fell asleep. Even though I tried to convince myself that it was just another dream I could feel my heart start to race again. Just like before, I squinted and relaxed my eyes to calm myself. When I finally opened my eyes I saw it was still dark around me. I decided to try to go back to sleep.

All of a sudden I heard some strange noises—then strange voices. I got scared again because when I opened my eyes I saw that it still pitch dark everywhere. With a small thud, I felt like the floating stopped and I came to a rest. I didn't know what to think. My heart began to race out of control when I suddenly smelled the scent of pine trees again. Was I in that field again? I didn't know what to do so I stayed real quiet in my bed and tried to go back to sleep. I decided to patiently wait for daylight to appear. It seemed like the night was lasting forever.

Unexpectedly, I heard a strange noise above me. Like the sky over me had lifted, I was surrounded by bright lights. I had to squint my eyes again to focus and try to figure out what was happening. A stronger smell of pine surrounded me. To my right, left and everywhere around me were faces that I did not recognize. I had no idea who they were or where I was. Then someone strange bent down and picked me up. Now my heart was beating faster than ever. I was so scared.

Then they gently stroked and caressed me. It felt so heavenly that I just melted in their arms. Then others came to see me and they were just as kind. Was this for real or was I dreaming? I didn't really know but it felt so wonderful that it did not make a difference and I hoped it would last forever.

Moments later I was put down on the floor. It was a strange sensation. It was so soft and plush. My feet had never felt anything this good before. I was no longer confined to a small space or to my bed. I was feeling freedom for the first time in my life. I was loving it. People came from all around to love on me. That made it even better.

The pine tree smell was coming from a huge tree decorated from top to bottom with lights and ornaments. It was such a beautiful sight and not scary any more.

My new friends gathered some presents from under the tree and opened them up for me. I got new bowls, a knitted sweater, a ball and some toys. Seven gifts to be exact, which they mentioned was the number of candles they lit at their Grandma's house during the holiday season they celebrated with her. I wanted to be pinched to make sure this was not a dream when I heard a voice say that I would never ever have to go back to the puppy mill—I had finally found a forever home.

Biography: Penni has always had a love for pets and would probably have a zoo if that was possible. She was born in Metropolis, Illinois (the official hometown of Superman). She moved to Virginia at an early age where she resided for the majority of her life. Upon her retirement from a twenty-year career with the Department of the Army, she returned to Illinois for five years before moving to Phoenix. She is a Mom to two daughters, Grandmom to six grandchildren and Great Grandmom to four great grandchildren. She is enjoying her retirement years with her oldest grandson, Matthew, a menagerie of show cats and a Chihuahua named Chiquita. She enjoys volunteer work (especially at book stores), crocheting, the cat fancy and collecting signed books.

"A house is not a home without a pet." ~ Anonymous

"An animal's eyes have the power to speak a great language." ~ Martin Buber

THE PUPPY'S CHRISTMAS GIFT

By Kriel

I'm getting a present today,
I hope it goes my way,
to run and jump and play
in a home forever to stay!

I'll be good, I'll really try!
I'll be brave and try not to cry.
It's exciting, but I'll be a good guy!
Mama said I earned it, that's why!

I'll always remember this treat.
I'm so excited I can't keep my seat!
I'll try really hard to keep neat!
I'm getting a gift, I'll soon greet...

Will it be a girl or boy?
Oh, I'm getting such a great toy!
And its hugs will not annoy!
Open the lid! Don't be coy!!

It's a BOY! Into his arms I jump -
I lick his face and his nose I bump!
His laughter gives me such delight!
He's a great gift, they were right!!

Biography: Kriel is a 45 year old single mother living in Phoenix, AZ, since 2000. Prior to Phoenix she lived in Northern AZ for 18 years and all over CA for 17 years. She is an animal lover and always surrounds herself with many dogs and/or cats. She has also had mice, hamsters, lizards, fish galore and birds. Besides poetry, Kriel has a book or two in the works!

"Every boy should have two things: a dog, and a mother willing to let him have one." ~ Anonymous

"There is no psychiatrist in the world like a puppy licking your face." ~ Ben Williams

DO BIRDS THINK?

By Nancy Marshall

It was mid-august in the Prescott (AZ) National Forest. I looked up at a beam under the cabin roof to see a small nest. *Must be an abandoned nest,* I thought. Most of the birds have their babies in May and June and move on.

I reached to pick up the nest. It would make a great addition to my 'treasure trove' of empty bird nests, bones, quartz crystals, rusted horseshoes and feathers from wildlife.

To my surprise three little feathery babies huddled closely together in the nest. They were terrified. As I hastened to put their home back where it belonged, one youngster tried to escape and fluttered to the ground. What had I been thinking?

I heard a few short, delicate eep-eep's and spotted the mother in a nearby tree. "Eep…eep." She was trying to communicate.

The mom was a phoebe, with that distinctive crested head. She was so slender, just having given birth to the three eggs that had made her look so fluffy in the spring.

What was she saying? Was it "get out of here?" Could she have been saying, "Strange human, follow me?" But no, she flitted among the branches and stayed near her babies.

Was she calling to her baby on the ground, *I'm here, I'll help if I can, I won't leave you?* I think that's what she was thinking, because she stayed within ten feet of her baby.

Meanwhile, he huddled on the ground. He had not yet caught the hang of this flying thing. His mama had not pushed him over the edge peeping, "you're ready." He had jumped or fallen, due to my thoughtlessness. The chick was too young to fly, but there he was—out and on the ground.

I tried to catch him and return him to the nest. I enveloped him in two hands. But as I lifted him up, he flew off again. There he landed, back on the ground.

Clearly he was thinking, *I have to get away from her.*

Mom flitted from low branch to low branch. Obviously she was thinking, *I have to stay near my baby.*

Finally I realized that I was the problem. I moved away.

The chick fluttered, tried a hopping flight, and landed five feet down the path. Mom called an "eep" as she flew to a branch closer to him.

The Good Lord in His wisdom endowed humans with hands, so that we might scoop our babies up out of harm's way. But with the same wisdom, He appears to have decided that wings and a beak were better for the birds. So this mama bird couldn't scoop her child up and away from harm. She could only chirp and fly. The Good Lord has not told us whether, and to what extent, birds can think.

But I think she was thinking, *I have to stay with him until he can fly. He has his feathers, downy and scrawny. It's a little early, but maybe he can do it. Eep, eep.*

And so I left them, mother and chick, as he flutter-flew-hopped down the path and she flew close to him, encouraging him to fly.

Biography: Nancy Marshall has worked for several years in the Juvenile Court. She and her husband have a cabin in the Bradshaw Mountains, which is marked as a wildlife refuge for the animals who live there. She lives in Phoenix with two dogs and a cat.

"Birds sing after a storm; why shouldn't people feel free to delight in whatever remains to them?"
~ Rose F. Kennedy

PREPARING FOR HANUKAH

(Sub-titled: Obviously the butler was not Jewish)

Author Unknown

A Jewish couple in London won twenty million pounds in the lottery. They bought a magnificent mansion in Knightsbridge and surrounded themselves with all the material wealth imaginable.

They decided to hire a butler. They found the perfect butler through an agency, very proper and very British, and brought him back to their home.

The day after his arrival, he was instructed to set up the dining table for four, as they were inviting the Cohens to an intimate Hanukah celebration. The couple left the house to do some shopping.

When they returned, they found the table set for six. Perplexed, they asked the butler why it was set for six

 when they had expressly asked him to set it for four.

The butler replied, "The Cohens telephoned and said they were bringing the Blintzes."

CARING FOR SCOTTIE

By Lee Bisbey

I shivered with excitement and fright as Ray held me in his arms. I was a special Christmas delivery, a black and white terrier mix. When we arrived at my new home, he put me down and I scampered away and hid under the stairs. I peeked out from under the bottom stair and tottered over to where another giant was sitting. She reached down and picked me up. My tail wagged to and fro and that began our friendship.

"Let's call him Scottie," Ray said to his sister, Lee.

My owners learned not to pull my tail because that hurt and to watch where they walked so I would not have hurt paws.

My masters were loving but sometimes they used a "weapon" to housebreak me. My introduction to the rolled-up newspaper was one afternoon after I left a puddle on the kitchen floor. A deafening sound came from behind me. Then I felt a whack on my behind and Lee rushed me outside to the backyard. The newspaper didn't hurt me but it scared me half to death. My owners later learned that using the newspaper was not the best way to discipline me. A loud "NO" worked much better.

As a puppy, I needed to eat 3 to 4 times a day. Milk tasted good but very little was given to me. I ate mostly dry puppy food. Even though I begged for food at the kitchen table, Lee knew that giving me table scraps would hurt my stomach and make me fat.

Besides feeding me every day, Ray brushed me. Once a week he bathed me and checked me over for ticks, sores and swellings. Ray never found a tick but he noticed I scratched a lot. He took me to a doctor, a vet. He said I was allergic to Bermuda grass. The doctor gave me a shot to make me feel better. He checked my eyes which were bright and clear. He opened my mouth and it was pink like bubble gum. The vet said I was in excellent health and should visit him once a year for an annual checkup.

Visiting the vet was not one of my favorite things to do. I'd rather ride in Lee's car with my head outside the window so that a breeze could blow through my fur. Whether I rode in Lee's car or took long walks, I always wore my collar that had my dog tags attached telling who I was and where I lived. Once I ran away from home to chase a cat. It teased me by standing in front of me at my backyard fence. Dirt flew everywhere as I dug my way out to run after the cat. She disappeared and I did not know where I was.

"Here nice doggie," my neighbor said patting my head, "I'll take you home right away."

I was so glad my owners never took my collar off except to wash me. My tags were on the collar and I didn't stay lost for very long. Life around the Bisbeys has certainly been different since I came to stay. My owners learned that I was not a stuffed toy that lives on a shelf or sits on a bed. I require care and training. But after all, how many stuffed animals do you know that greet you at the back door with a wagging tail and slurpy kiss?

Biography: Leonora Bisbey goes by the pen name Lee Bisbey. She is retired from the Military (Navy & Army National Guard) and Civil Service. Her hobbies include writing, board games and the computer. She is a graduate of the Children's Literature Institute and a member of the writing group at Washington Activity Center. She is published in the National Library of Poetry, Veterans' Voices and North Phoenix Baptist Singles newsletters. She has two Chihuahuas, Tera and Victor. She believes you can learn so much about life from your pets.

"My little dog—a heartbeat at my feet." ~ Edith Wharton

ᘓᘒ

"Dogs are not our whole life, but they make our lives whole." ~ Roger Caras

---

ᘓᘒ

"The dog represents all that is best in man." ~ Etienne Charlet

A DIFFERENT LOVE STORY

By Lisa Fisk

I remember the day I met my mistress clearly. It was love at first sight. When I spotted her, I did everything I could to get her to look at me. I played it cool, smiled and made eyes at her. Confidence works. She took one look at my sleek, well-muscled body, brown eyes and long lashes, and she was hooked. We went home together twenty minutes later. Neither of us ever looked back. We've been committed to each other for six years.

Sure, I know what the others were saying, *Why him? What's he got that we haven't got?* Nothing really. It was a matter of picking her out from the crowd and focusing my powers to get her to cross the room and realize she was in love.

When Julie and I became partners for life, as I like to think of it, it was the two of us against the world. Before you could say "Bob's your uncle" we established territory and routines. Come to think of it, maybe that's why she named me Bob. She pays the bills and pampers me to the best of her ability; I do all of the things she won't do for herself.

Oh, you might think that I've got it easy and I don't take my responsibilities to her seriously. I do. Just because I'm a terrier-poodle mix doesn't mean that I don't have responsibilities. For the last six years, I've protected her from untold numbers of cats who wanted to use her flowers as a sandbox, numerous newspapers that were in danger of being unopened and unread, and every delivery person who has knocked on our door.

My most solemn responsibility? Kitchen duty. I lay in front of the stove whenever she's cooking. If I'm not there, she might forget to stir something and then I have to deal with the burned odor that stays in the air for hours. Not only do I keep the floor next to the stove warm, which is surely why it works as well as it does, but I am in charge of quality control. Just the other night she made stir-fried vegetables and she forgot to use the glaze. After she slipped me a piece of celery, which did NOT meet the taste test, my expression alone led her to realize what she'd forgotten and correct the dish.

What's the worst of my many jobs? The Christmas letter. The Christmas letter is the worst of all the torments put together. Julie spends days going over all of my adventures for the year: the men I've nipped at, the garbage I examined for tantalizing tidbits while sunning myself on the living room carpet, the trips to the dog park to introduce her to new people. After she has put the epic together, she won't mail it unless there's a picture of yours truly in a Santa suit included.

Normally, I'll pose all day long for pictures provided that she's got little liver treats or hot dog bits for me. I can look adorable for hours on end when I don't have to get all dressed up and be trotted in front of a stranger who doesn't know a hill of beans about good dog biscuits and then puts me in the arms of a stranger in a matching red suit. To make matters worse, my little Santa suit binds under the arms and the hat tends to flop into my eyes so I can't see clearly.

Once everyone thinks I look properly cute, the photographer talks baby-talk to me until I pay attention. Sometimes I'm there, being touched and fondled by a strange man for several minutes. It's degrading. The year I wiggled so much she had to sit on Santa's lap so she could hold me still began a series of pictures together.

That particular Christmas she got Mitch. It turned out that he was in the costume and he liked how she wiggled on his lap so much he tried to take her home that very day.

Normally, I'm a very sharing kind of a dog. I share my tennis ball at the park with the humans who forget to bring toys for their puppies. I would share any cats I find in the backyard with Julie; I did it once and her screams were deafening. I let her put her head on my pillow at night. I even let her use most of the blankets on the bed because when she gets cold, no one sleeps well and I look awful when I get bags under my eyes.

Sharing with Mitch is a horse of a different color. He doesn't divvy up his table scraps. He has a misguided notion that a pillow should only comfort one head at a time. The first time he slept with us, he got Julie so cold she made miserable noises. Doesn't he understand that when Julie doesn't sleep no one does? Every time I tried to perform my valet service of acting as his personal towel warmer, he made unkind comments about the color of my fur and acted like I might have fleas. Fleas? Please. Julie takes me to the groomer once a month and I have never ever had a flea much less a tick.

The first Christmas with Mitch, Julie did help me get my own back. Mitch came over and saw the tree she set up in the living room with all of the glorious presents under it and examined them. Each package had been wrapped carefully and had a coordinating bow on top.

"Are these all for me, Julie?" Mitch asked with a smile. "We haven't been dating all that long."

Two weeks. They'd only been dating two weeks and he thought everything beneath the tree was for him. The nerve.

"Course not." She picked me up and held me close to her chest. My favorite spot. I get a much better view of the room from there. "They're all for Bob."

"Bob? All of this for one dog?"

"Sure." She covered my ears with her hands. "He needed some new squeaky toys and he wore out his special cushion. And I found the cutest—"

"But he's just a dog."

Just a dog? Excuse me? Just. A. Dog.

"Who do you buy presents for?" she asked.

"My parents, my brother, a couple of friends. I'm hoping maybe to buy one for you." He smiled at her.

"My point exactly. You buy presents for people you love. People who mean something to you. Right?"

"Yes. But he's—"

"He's my best friend. He's the one male in my life who's never let me down and loves me just like I am. He doesn't criticize me and I think he's perfect."

Actually, I do point out when dinner is late by running in little circles back and forth from the den to my bowl in the kitchen. Once in a while, I let her know our walks haven't been long enough by nibbling on the end of the night shirt she leaves on the floor when she's in a hurry to go to work. If she ever forgets completely about feeding me, we'll have to have some serious negotiations about the future of our relationship. For now, so far, so good.

"How can I get favored nation status?" Mitch asked. "I can think of a few things I might do better than the dog." He smiled broadly as he picked up one of the packages and sniffed at it.

"All of the food items are on top of the fridge so he won't get into them early."

"Then what's that?"

She shrugged. "Probably his Christmas ornament."

She got me a new one every year. My favorite is the bone with my name written on it.

"I hope you didn't hear that, Bob."

"Put the dog down and we'll see if I don't do at least one thing better than he does." Mitch closed the distance between them and extracted me from my mistress's arms and deposited me on the floor. He cupped her cheek and kissed her.

I was fine with him kissing her until she started to make noises like she was in pain. Then I became Bob, Dog of Action. I grabbed his pants leg and began to tug and pull until he let her go.

"Bob. Bob, it's okay," Julie said as she bent down to extract the fabric from my mouth.

"He seems jealous. Maybe he should have a playmate of his own."

"It's part of his job to keep me away from the big bad wolf." She scratched my ears and said, "That's my best boy."

"Definitely he should have a playmate of his own."

And that is how Millie the cocker spaniel mix came to live with us at Easter, but that's another story.

TALES & TAILS

Biography: Lisa Fisk and her husband are currently owned by a golden retriever mix, Thunder. They are living their happily ever after in Scottsdale, Arizona.

"He doesn't reckon his dog has human feelings, but he sure lets you know when you hurt his instincts." ~ Robert Brault

ॐ

"Most pets display so many humanlike traits and emotions it's easy to forget they're not gifted with the English language and then get snubbed when we talk to them and they don't say anything back." ~ Stephenie Geist

ॐ

"You enter into a certain amount of madness when you marry a person with pets." ~ Nora Ephron

ODE TO DR. CARASTRO

By James F. Weinsier

(My dog's eye surgeon, Dr. Carastro performed an operation that connected Eleanor's salivary glands to her eyes—keeping them moist. The operation gave Eleanor sight for three years—'til her passing.)

Every once in a while,
Someone comes into your life,
And implants all their genius
With the skill of a surgeon's knife.

They not only touch an ailing part,
Wherever that may be,
But cut themselves into your heart
And root, just like a tree.

I have met such a person,
And see her in my dreams,
And now, when I awake,
I can *see* my master's beams.

Biography: James was born in New York City and raised on Long Island. He is a Navy veteran. He has degrees from Nassau Community College and the University of Miami. He began grappling with writing in 1966 and published *Here...and Afterthoughts* and *More...Thoughts*. His latest publication from 2006 is titled, *Where Do We Go?* James is now retired and lives with his wife in Fernandina Beach, FL.

IT'S NOT SIZE THAT MATTERS: IT'S SENSITIVITY

By Nancy Marshall

It was October. We arrived at our cabin in the Bradshaws after sunset to find a group of trespassers – horseback riders – cooking their Dinty Moore beef stew over an outside fire. We said they could stay if they would share their dinner with us. Of course they did.

The next morning they let us take a short ride up the dry creek bed with two of their horses. My husband's horse, in the lead, turned and ascended quickly and powerfully out of the creek bed, up the bank, onto a trail. My horse turned to follow, lost her balance, and fell on her right side, crushing my leg. As she shook her startled self free from me, she strove to land all four hooves away from this human she had mistakenly harmed.

Regaining her balance, she stood a few feet away, a look of fear in her eyes. Despite our inter-species language barrier, I understood that she was afraid of what she had done wrong and was afraid to continue. I realized I had to be the one in charge. "It's ok, lady, we're both ok. I won't ride you just now, but I do have to lead you up the bank. Ready?" She timidly followed me. I loosened the reins and prodded her forward. She lumbered up the rocky slope. Walking by her side, I patted her neck. She calmed down. She was begging me to forgive her, to make things all right. The Great Interspecies Spirit had allowed me to hear her voice.

"A canter is the cure for all evil." ~ Benjamin Disraeli

"A horse gallops with his lungs, perseveres with his heart, and wins with his character." ~ Tesio

"Who can believe that there is no soul behind those luminous eyes!" ~ Theophile Gautier

OZZIE THE WONDER DOG

By Thomas J. Lambke

W e have always been dog people. Ever since our kids were babies our family has always included a canine friend. Our first dog was a Springer Spaniel named Mickey, also known as Lambke's Lord of Michelob! Mickey was a great guy who didn't mind when the kids leapt from the couch onto his back. He loved to go for walks, was very well-behaved and had a great disposition. He had this cool looking black line above his lip that looked like a moustache and we had friends who called him Groucho! Mickey was an amazing guy who could leap and run all day and still had time for kisses. Sadly, we had to let Mickey go in January, 2001, after having shared fourteen years of loving companionship.

We realized it would be hard to replace Mickey but we tried anyway. We even bought another Springer that we named Gonzo, after the star of the Arizona Diamondbacks, Luis Gonzalez. He had quite a different temperament and we had to adjust to his unique personality. Just as we were getting used to him, Gonzo was diagnosed with epilepsy and within a few months he had a severe seizure and passed away. We were so traumatized that I wasn't sure if we would ever want another dog. In the summer of 2005, my brother, Ken, called and told me he wanted to give me a special gift for my upcoming 50th birthday. He knew we missed having a dog around and asked if we would consider a German Shepherd. Ken and his family have had a Shepherd for several years and Gracie seemed like a good girl. However, I have always been rather leery of the breed and was never that comfortable when meeting a Shepherd. As a matter of fact, having been a letter carrier for twenty years, I had experienced my share of dog scares but had only been bitten once, by a German Shepherd named Spike!

After discussing my brother's offer with my wife and kids, we decided we wanted a dog badly enough to try a Shepherd. Our confidence was increased just knowing that the breeder was quite reliable and came with my brother's seal of approval. But my wife, Karen, made it very clear that he was to be MY dog. Ken, however, then disclosed an important fact about this particular Shepherd; he had only three legs! It seems when he was just six weeks old someone stepped on one of his back paws and caused a blood clot. Because he was part of a litter sired by an award-winning 140 pound stud, the vet wanted to put him to sleep, thinking it would be hard to find a home for him. Luckily, the breeder asked for time to make some calls, talked to my brother, who in turn talked to me, and we agreed to give him a home. Ken assured us that the puppy had already undergone surgery, was just finishing eight weeks of physical therapy, and was ready to be shipped from Illinois. Because our son, Bryan, who was born with Down syndrome and created a fair share of challenges for us, we figured a dog with a disability would simply be a different kind of challenge.

Although we now live in Arizona, my family is originally from the suburbs of Chicago, and I have been a White Sox fan my entire life. So choosing a name for our new pet was fairly easy. The manager of the White Sox, Ozzie Guillen, was a man who faced adversity and challenges every day, so the three-legged addition to our family became OZZIE. Along with Bryan, this brave animal has changed our lives with his incredible courage and will to live.

My brother shipped Ozzie to us via Dallas but the weather was so bad in Texas, he was rerouted from Dallas to Albuquerque and then, finally to Phoenix, during an Arizona monsoon. When I picked him up at one in the morning, all I saw were a pair of big ears on top of a scrawny, coyote-looking animal that looked nothing like a Shepherd! As I approached the dog crate I softly called his name. His ears immediately perked up and he looked right at me. Luckily I knew that Ken had already been calling him that or it would have freaked me out. I took Ozzie home to meet the rest of the family and we made him comfortable.

From the get-go, Ozzie was unbelievable, in both good ways and bad. When I took him for walks, he would find a way to get loose and I would have to run him down. And boy, could he run! The guy doesn't even know he's supposed to have four legs and he runs as if he has five. If I was working outside and used the side gate, he would somehow escape and I would search the neighborhood until I found him, usually three or four blocks away. Ozzie is very outgoing and loves to meet people. It is the other dogs he seems to have problems with.

I initially tried taking Ozzie to local dog parks. He was actually fairly well-behaved the first few times, content to chase a ball and sniff to his heart's content. But one time a couple of smaller dogs decided it was okay to pester him. I think they might have sensed a weakness because of his missing leg. He put up with them for a while but then finally had enough and turned on them, baring his ferocious-looking teeth. He did not bite them but he sure scared the living daylights out of them! And I pity any dog who dares to chase his ball down. I have had to pull him off several would-be brave dogs! But let's face it; there is proper etiquette to follow when at a dog park and unfortunately, most dogs still have masters that do not pay enough attention to them, and that is when problems arise.

Ozzie is very protective, especially in our house. If anyone as much as walks by outside, his bark lets us all know. He has always been and is still extremely curious about anyone that we allow into the house, but continues to believe they are only visiting to play ball with him! Before we let someone in, we have to make sure that they understand that he is a Shepherd and ask if they are afraid of big dogs, because he can be quite scary. I would not want to be that person who decides to break into our home for fear of what Ozzie may do. He is now around eighty-five pounds of muscle and even without a leg, it does not slow him down a bit!

Ozzie loves to go for walks but he cannot go very far without tiring. He likes to just plop down to rest a couple of times each walk and fully expects me to allow him that time. He loves to roll onto his back and have his belly rubbed and scratched and it is rather humorous to see his stump flail about with excitement! I enjoy the feedback that I get from others who see or meet him for the first time, especially when they are surprised to discover that he only has three legs.

In my wildest dreams I would never have thought I would invite a German Shepherd to kiss my face. But I taught Ozzie that to get his daily milk bone he has to sit, give a paw to shake, and give me a kiss. I think it's ironic that I now allow a dog of this breed to slobber my face considering my history with shepherds! One hot day I discovered Ozzie loves ice cubes. We cannot even fix ourselves a drink using ice cubes without him racing over begging for a cube. Just the tingling sound of the cubes falling into a glass will send him into a dither!

Since he is now going on six, we realize Ozzie will continue to slow down even more and have prepared ourselves to be his caregivers in the future. Until then, we truly enjoy his companionship and marvel at his ability to change how others think. Most people are amazed at how well he gets around on only three legs while others are encouraged by his courage and heart.

My family is blessed to have had the lifelong opportunity of experiencing the joys of raising our son, Bryan, and teaching others about Down syndrome. We feel doubly blessed to have shared similar experiences because of Ozzie and his disability. Because of the knowledge we have gained from Ozzie and Bryan, my entire family has become advocates for people and animals with disabilities and we enjoy using that understanding to promote awareness and tolerance in everyone we meet.

Biography: Tom and his family live in Chandler, AZ. He has been married for 33 years to his high school sweetheart, Karen. He authored *Spirit, Courage and Resolve ... a Special Olympics Athlete's Road to Gold* ([www.spiritcouragerésolve.com](www.spiritcourageresolve.com)) describing the experiences with and because of their son, Bryan, who has Down syndrome. It is the story of Bryan's road to becoming an International Special Olympics gold medal winner at the World Games in Ireland. He and Bryan co-authored *I Just Am ... a Story of Down Syndrome Awareness and Tolerance* (www.ijustam) as a tool to educate the public about the disability. Tom and Bryan are also both past members of the Advisory Board of Best Buddies Arizona.

Bryan and Ozzie
Photo by Linda F. Radke,
Five Star Publications, Inc.

PILGRIM

By Ellen H. Calvert

As I grew older, I began to really value this family of mine. They were a very generous group and I vowed to find a way to be just as generous.

Prowling the neighborhood one warm December night in Tempe, I spied a young female kitten sitting on the wall, three houses down the street. She "meowed" at my approach and I "meowed" in return. I was filled with the holiday spirit.

Looking at the colored lights that decorated the neighborhood homes, I decided to honor the importance of sharing by bringing her home with me. I signaled her to "follow me." She sweetly followed me home and barely maneuvered her tiny body through the pet door. Although it was a stretch for her little legs, she followed my role modeling and managed to tumble into the kitchen.

Once inside, I walked her over to my special place where two brown pottery dishes containing water and food rested on a blue placemat. I had left enough of my dinner for a late snack which I now offered her. Daintily nibbling on my organic dry food, she purred her pleasure while I stood by. I was pleasantly surprised at how good sharing felt.

Noise from the other room alerted me that someone was still awake and watching television. No problem there. It was still early and the night was young.

All of a sudden, the kitchen light switched on and a surprised Nick surveyed the scene. A smile crept across Nick's face as he viewed me and my new companion. Immediately, I was struck by how much I really loved this kid, as all six feet three inches of him looked down on us.

"Whoa, what's this all about? Pilgrim, what's going on here and who's your new little friend?" Nick asked, acting very paternal.

Then, Nick took a few steps back. "Mom, I know you're in bed, but this you have to see. Pilgrim's brought home a little kitten that is busily eating the food in his dish," Nick called, "you've got to see this to believe it! I don't know how the kitten made it in."

"So-o-o, Pilgrim now has his own kitten. Is that what I'm hearing?" commented Ellen, entering the room.

"No, I think Pilgrim had a date and brought her home afterward to 'raid' his dish for a late night snack," laughed Nick.

While patiently enduring their humorous bantering back and forth, I felt that I had exhibited a new found maturity in this situation.

After my new feline friend finished eating, I noticed that the main door had been opened to make it easier for us to leave (and have some privacy, peace, and quiet). Both Nick and Ellen continued their conversation about my "ulterior motives" in adopting my own kitten, sharing my food during the holidays, and the odds of that happening.

Exiting the house, the last comment I heard was that I was really sweet in sharing my food and something about me that never ceased to amaze them.

Biography: Ellen Hasenecz Calvert resides in her adopted home state of Arizona. Born in New Jersey, Ellen considered herself a "Joisey" girl until 1988 when she fell in love with the land, the culture, the people, and the fragile beauty of the Southwest. While living in Albuquerque, New Mexico, Ellen wrote her first book, *Pilgrim, Tales of a Traveling Cat*, from inside the head of the family cat. The book was published in 2009 and Ellen can be reached on her website www.ellencalvert.com.

"A cat is a puzzle for which there is no solution." ~ Hazel Nicholson

"Dogs have owners, cats have staff." ~ Anonymous

FEETIE PAJAMAS

By John Green

Once, in a time that never was, and never will be again, the only kind of pajamas that boys and girls had to wear were feetie pajamas. You know, the kind of pajamas where the feet are part of the pants. Some liked their feetie pajamas. But many did not.

There was a little boy in that time, who lived with his mother and father and little sister, who was one of the many who did not.

One night his mother and father had to go out for the evening to care for a sick aunt.

"You two get into your pajamas", they said to the children. "We won't be gone very long."

The father said to the little boy, "Be sure to take good care of your sister while we're gone…and don't leave the house!" With that, the mother and father put on their coats and hurried off into the night.

At first all went very well. The little boy and his sister played some games and put on their feetie pajamas (even though they didn't like them one little bit). But after a while, the little girl began to feel very sick. The little boy did everything he could think of to help her feel better, but she only felt worse and worse.

He tried giving her some soup. He bundled her warm under the quilt of her bed. He sang her quiet little songs. But when he felt her forehead as he had seen his mother do, she felt very, very warm. He knew then, that she had

a fever and he began to get very scared. He had to get the doctor for his sister. And he had to do it fast!

Now this was in the days long before there were telephones, or even the idea that there might ever be such a thing. And the only doctor he knew of lived on the other side of town. But the little boy loved his sister very much, so without even taking the time to get dressed he ran out of the house into the night to fetch the doctor.

The night was cold and wet, but he ran very fast over the rough cobblestone streets because the only thing that

mattered to him was getting to the doctor just as fast as he could. And as he ran the feet on his feetie pajamas began to get ripped and torn.

On and on he ran.

As he passed a neighbor's fence, he decided to take a short-cut by jumping over the fence and cutting through their yard. But no sooner had he gotten over the fence, he remembered the fierce watchdogs that lived on the other side. Growling and snapping, they chased him across the yard. As he scrambled up the fence on the other side, one of the dogs managed to take a bite out of the toe of one of the feet of his feetie pajamas. Fortunately, he missed the boy's toes. Puffing and panting, the little boy kept on running. And as he ran, the feet on his feetie pajamas became more and more torn.

Soon he came upon the small stream that ran through the center of town. The bridge was very far away and would be much too far out of his way. The stream was shallow, so he decided to wade across. The sharp rocks and pebbles of the streambed tore at the feet of his feetie pajamas, but he didn't care. All that mattered to him, was getting the doctor.

Reaching the other side, he ran on and on, over the rough cobblestone streets. By the time he got to the doctor's house, there wasn't much left of the feet of his feetie pajamas. But he hadn't much time to think about that. Quickly he knocked at the door.

After what seemed to be a very long time passed, the boy feared that the doctor might not be home. Just as he was about to give up, the door swung open, and there was the doctor in his robe carrying a lantern.

Looking sleepily at the boy the doctor exclaimed, "I know you. You're the little boy that lives on the other side of town. What brings you here so late at night?"

The boy explained that his little sister was very, very sick. "Please," said the boy, "you must come with me quickly!"

The kindly doctor fetched his bag, and brought the boy back to the stable. As he hitched his horse to his buggy he said, "You are a very brave little boy to run all this way in the night. You must love your sister very much."

They drove through town as fast as they could. Soon they arrived at the boy's house and hurried inside. The doctor took one look at the little boy's sister and exclaimed, "It's a good thing you came to me when you did, for your sister is indeed very sick. I have some medicine in my bag that will make her feel better, but you had best wait out in the living room while I look after her."

The boy did as he was told. He had no sooner sat down however, when his mother and father returned.

They took one look at him, and the torn and tattered remains of the feet of his feetie pajamas and became very, very angry.

"Where have you been?" cried his mother.

"I thought I told you to stay in the house," shouted his father.

"And just look at the feet on your feetie pajamas," exclaimed his mother.

Before the boy could even start to explain, the doctor came out of his sister's room. He told the boy's parents the whole story. Their anger quickly turned to pride as they hugged and kissed him. "You have a very

brave and quick thinking little boy here," said the doctor. "His sister will be fine now, but if he hadn't come to me as quickly as he did, there is no telling what might have happened. But those feet on his feetie pajamas sure are a mess. I think I might have a cure for that as well."

The doctor reached into his bag, took out a sharp pair of scissors, and cut off the remains of the feet of the feetie pajamas. "There now," he said, "that ought to do the trick!" He patted the boy on the back, bid his parents good night, and left just as quickly as he had come.

And soon, a very tired boy was sleeping soundly in his bed.

That is not the end of the story…

The very next day, the doctor told his housekeeper all about the little boy, and what he had done.

The housekeeper told the baker.

The baker told the miller.
The miller told the postman.

The postman told the

clerk …and so the story spread all through the town.

Very soon the tale reached the ear of the Burgermeister. Now the

Burgermeister (that's another word for Mayor, but a much better title for a story like this) had never heard of such courage from such a little boy in the town in all its long history. "Something must be done to celebrate such a heroic feat," he exclaimed. "Let there be a great holiday next Tuesday. There should be feasting and dancing and music," he decreed. *And maybe even a speech or two,* he thought to himself. The burgermeister could not resist an opportunity to hear himself talk.

And so it was arranged. On the given day, the whole town turned out in the village common to honor the little boy for his daring courage. People ate and danced and the town band played music from dawn 'til dusk. At long last, after all the speeches were given, the Burgermeister called the little boy up to the bandstand. He praised the boy and offered that the town would grant him anything he desired to reward him for his bravery.

"Now what is it you would like?" asked the Burgermeister of the boy.

The boy thought of all the things that would be nice to have. *A new pair of skates? A pony? Perhaps a toy store of his very own!* It can be really hard to decide what you want, when you can have anything.

As he thought, he looked out into the crowd. There he saw all the boys and girls of the town. It was so late that some of the real little ones were already in their pajamas, and ready for bed. Feetie pajamas, of course. It was then that he thought of the feetie pajamas, and how so many of the children wished they didn't have to wear them. He thought of his own pajamas that no longer had feet. He had asked his mother not to sew on new ones, and because she was so proud of him, she had agreed.

So he turned to the Burgermeister and said, "I would like…I would like…," he stammered, "that any boy or girl who doesn't like to wear feetie pajamas, could have the feet cut off just like mine."

At first, the Burgermeister was dumbfounded. Then he smiled broadly and said, "What little surprise, that such a brave and thoughtful boy should have such an unselfish request. So it shall be by law," he decreed, "that from now and forever more, any boy or girl who doesn't want feet on their feetie pajamas may bring them at any time to the town hall and have them cut off!"

And so it came to pass, that there would at last be a choice of pajama bottoms, and before long, the idea had spread from town to town, city to city and all throughout the world.

And just what, might you ask, happened to all the feet that were cut off those feetie pajamas? Mothers thought they might become nice dust rags. And fathers thought they might be nice golf club covers. But at last a better idea took hold. To reward all good little boys and girls, every year at Christmas time they were hung up by the fireplace in hopes that Saint Nicholas might fill them with toys!

Biography: John was born in 1953 in Schenectady, New York. He graduated from the Rochester Institute of Technology with Painting/Illustrating as his major. After working for an advertising agency for 10 years, he opened his own graphic design and illustration firm which has been in operation since 1985. (www.creativecolleagues.com).

  John has been married to his lovely wife, Cathy for over 26 years and they have been in business together for nearly as long. She spent many years as an accountant, business manager for Creative Colleagues and as a certified pre-school teacher at Desert Springs Pre-School & Kindergarten. Books and children are her passion in life. Planning, combined with their existing entrepreneurial spirit finally came together with the opening of a children's book store, Tikes & Tales, in Phoenix in 2010. (www.tikesandtales.com).

  Copyrighted by John in 2002, "Feetie Pajamas" started out and continues as a "told tale" that John conjured up and told to his two sons when they were little. He continues to redefine, refine and adapt it today at Tikes & Tales story events.

EDITOR'S NOTE: It is with great sadness to announce that John's beloved wife, Cathy, passed away on October 25, 2010, after fighting a courageous battle with cancer. She will be sorely missed by all. See *TRIBUTE TO CATHY GREEN, Heaven-bound October 25, 2010,* that follows.

TRIBUTE TO CATHY GREEN
Heaven-bound October 25, 2010

By Penni Ferry

C is for Cathy
Caring
Charming
Compassionate
Christian
Courageous to the end

A is for Ambitious
Admirable
Altitudinally challenged (John's
fancy words for being short)
Amicable
Athletic
An avid reader
An angel to watch over us

T is for Truthful
Trustworthy
Thankful
Tennis player
Thoughtful
Trooper
Trainer and teacher for many

H is for Hard worker
Honest
Helpful
Homemaker
Humble
Honorable
Heart warming
Happiness you brought to others

Y is for You
A great wife, mother, daughter,
sister, aunt and friend to many.
Thank you for touching each of our
lives in your own special way.
Thank you for your legacy that others
may now continue your dream.
Last, but certainly not least, thank
you for being you.

MY FAMILY CHILDHOOD

By Kriel

Sugar Cookies and Ginger Snaps
Cranberry and Popcorn strings
All kinds of paper wraps
and other lovely things.

Pumpkin, Pecan or Mincemeat
everyone I know vies -
You're in for a great treat -
Pies Pies Pies

There's sure to be food galore,
Turkey and potatoes,
and all the folklore,
then to service everyone goes.

Singing Christmas songs
Students out of class,
people attend in throngs,
going to midnight mass.

All the people decorating
tinsel everywhere
and ornaments hanging,
for awhile, the world without a care.

YOUNG LOVE

By Sven Rosckowff

Our first Christmas was spent fulfilling family obligations. Although we had a lofty corner apartment, our cozy first place together, we each waved at the other as our respective family-packed sedans pulled up to cart us off for a night of jubilation. The snowfall had broken off, providing a moment's respite as I walked you to the car. I knew better than to repeat my inquiry as to why we're parting, if only for a few hours, you'd shorn my rebellious locks a month earlier, but perhaps I was yet not presentable in my then present form.

"Don't wait up, I might stay down at my parents' house tonight, I just don't know."

"Alright, but I think I'll see you later though."

"No. Don't make me feel like I can't spend some time on my own."

You handed me your half-smoked Marlboro red and told me to wait back at the main entrance while you walked the short distance to a car idling at the corner. In the absence of your companionship I took in the vivid lighting surrounding your winter-clothed form.

Orange halogen street lamps had turned the snow banks into citrus sorbet, the busy street provided a light show of headlights, shadows jumping from tall, stone churches to ancient row houses, the gas station fluorescents settled on your scarf and proud shoulders. You turned and waved; I raised one hand high and used the other hand to smoke your cigarette.

We'd been together almost a year and things were going smoothly. I'd chased off the flock of competition biding for your attention, kept my cool, and had been ready for any more. You had seen me at my worst already, repeatedly, and finding my willingness to learn, allowed me to learn, to earn your respect.

ℛℒ

Fast-forward 4,000 days: Christmas gatherings, laughter-filled moments. In lieu of icy streets, car-exhaust encapsulated within clear, hardened piles of frozen precipitation, this morning the sun rises over sun-baked vistas, parched and vibrating with anticipation, awaiting soon-to-come torrential wetness.

Bodies hum with caffeine, pools of energy 50-miles in diameter, and a vibrant playground dizzy with Christmas-time activity. Millions of modern day crusaders falling into concentrated packs as directed by coupons and advertisements. You are up early and kissing me softly on my face.

"Thank you for the earrings baby."

"Pillaging for presents were you? Well go ahead, put them on."

"I love you."

"I love you more."

"Merry Christmas."

"A very Merry Christmas!"

Biography: Sven is the Owner-operator of Bards Books. He resides in Phoenix with his loving wife and soul mate Leeann and their two cats, the lilth Lady Estelle and Snorri the Ancient Scavenger. He is an avid artist, musician and writer. In 2005, he authored his first novel, *Whispered Worlds*.

> "The cat has nine lives: three for playing, three for straying, three for staying." ~ Proverb

> "The cat lives alone, has no need of society, obeys only when she pleases, pretends to sleep that she may see more clearly, and scratches everything on which she can lay her paw." ~ François R. Chateaubriand

> "I am in favor of animal rights as well as human rights. That is the way of a whole human being." ~ Abraham Lincoln

A MID-WINTER'S TAIL

Bonus scene from *A Woman of Choice*

by Kris Tualla

February 1, 1820
Cheltenham
Missouri Territory

T he weak winter sun could not gain much ground
against clouds so low that they hid the treetops.
The world was cold, gray and muffled. Nicolas
Hansen cast a wary eye skyward as he and his foreman
John worked in the stable.

"It's coming, John. Let's get ready," he said.

The men mucked out the stalls and laid an extra layer
of fresh straw. They pulled down bales of hay from the
loft and stacked them by the doors. John made certain
the sheep were in the keep with plenty of straw and hay.

Four or five snowstorms came through Missouri each
winter, dumping several inches of heavy, wet snow.
This was shaping up to be a blizzard, with winds that
stole the breath and stung the faces of those who braved
it.

Addie recognized the signs as well. The housekeeper
and Nicolas's six-year-old son Stefan carried supplies
from the root cellar. Nicolas stacked extra wood on the
back porch to keep it dry and accessible.

Large flakes drifted out of the sky, blown in crazy

paths by the freshening wind. As the day aged, the wind strengthened. By afternoon, it keened through leafless trees, moaned over tops of chimneys and clattered shutters. The horizontal flurries were so thick, they could not see beyond the front porch. It was dangerous to go outside, even to the privy.

Nicolas, his new wife Sydney, and the children spent their time in the drawing room. The heavy curtains were closed to dampen drafts that seeped through the window casements. Nicolas pulled out his fiddle and passed more than an hour with his playful fiddling. When he stopped, baby Kirstie started to cry.

"Play your fiddle again," Sydney requested.

Nicolas obliged and Kirstie stopped crying. As long as Nicolas played, his infant daughter was quiet. When he paused, she wailed.

"Well, I'll be dashed," he mused. "I have ruined her early."

Addie baked throughout the day to pass time. John sat in the warm kitchen with his wife and repaired bridles, harnesses and other tack. The mingled smells of yeasty bread, cinnamon, coffee and saddle soap added to the scent of pine sap burning in the fireplaces. The manor smelled like a home.

The storm continued to blow into the night. Nicolas ventured out a few times to shovel snow from the root cellar door, in part to keep it from collapsing under the weight of the snow, and in part to make certain they could get to their food supply. After the supper dishes were washed, Nicolas cleared the snow off the cellar for the last time before bed.

He stomped through the back door in a cloud of cold air and blowing snow. Addie handed him a cup of coffee. He sipped the hot liquid, and used the cup to warm his cold-reddened hands.

"I believe it's slowing. It's merely blowing what's already on the ground."

Thump.

Scratch.

Addie looked at Nick. "And what do you suppose that was?"

The scratch came again, barely discernable over the raucous storm. Nicolas crossed to the door. "Whatever it is, it wants to be in here, not out there. And I truthfully cannot blame it a bit!"

He palmed his dirk and opened the back door. A large, hairy, four-legged creature stumbled in and collapsed on the floor.

Addie eased forward. "Is that supposed to be a dog? Or a wolf?"

Nicolas eyed the beast. "It's no wolf. So I reckon it's a dog. And a nearly dead one at that."

Thinking to ease its final hour, Nicolas picked up the enormous mass of hair and ice and carried it to the drawing room. He laid it on the floor with its back to the fire. It licked his hand.

The dog had large paws and a square head. His short, thick coat was buckskin, darkening around his muzzle and feet. He would stand about eight hands at the shoulder. He was so big Nicolas measured him in horse terms without realizing.

"*Pappa* what's that?" Stefan's eyes were round as dinner plates. "Can we keep it?"

Nicolas knelt beside the animal and began to pull impacted ice from between its toes. "His pads are black but I cannot discern if it's frostbite. If so, he'll likely not survive."

"He is very thin," Sydney ventured over Nicolas's shoulder. "I can see his ribs even through that mess of fur."

"He has missed a few meals, that's for certain. I wonder where he came from."

"*Pappa*, can you make him better?" Stefan's plea was punctuated by his grasp on Nicolas's shirt. "*Mamma* can help."

"We shall try, Stefan. But he may be too sick to save."

Stefan knelt next to Nicolas. "Can I do it, too?"

"Yes, son. See the ice between his toes? Get it out as gently as you can."

"I'll get wool fat and binding for his paws," Addie volunteered. "Don't know if he'll keep it on, but we can try." She headed to the kitchen for the supplies.

Nicolas slathered the thick grease on each paw and wrapped them with the cloth strips.

"What can we feed him, *Pappa*?"

"He's too weak to eat heavy." Nicolas pondered what might do. The dog began to whimper and wave his paws. But when he tried to stand, he yelped and fell to the floor. "His paws hurt. Addie, what can we give him for pain?"

"Willowbark tea is what I'd give a person," Addie answered.

"Can we brew some? Perchance mix it in some gravy from supper?" Sydney suggested.

"Well it certainly won't hurt him," Nicolas agreed.

Stefan petted the beast and that seemed to calm him, though he still waved his paws and whined. The smell of wet fur in front of the fire was so overpowering, Nicolas went to fetch some rags. He gave Stefan the task of rubbing the animal dry.

The women returned to the drawing room with the gravy and willowbark mixture. Nicolas sat on the floor, cradled the dog's head and held his jaws open. He stroked the beast's throat to make him swallow as Sydney dribbled the warm liquid into his mouth.

"Let him rest now," Nicolas said and laid the huge head on the floor. Stefan lay on the floor beside the creature. His tail lifted and dropped in a weak wag.

"What should we name him?" Stefan stroked the dog's ear.

"He'll tell us his name in due time," Nicolas said. "We shall wait for him." *Besides, the beast might yet die.*

"Can I sleep down here tonight, *Pappa*? So I can keep him company?"

Nicolas considered the animal. He was not a threat in his current condition and Stefan's presence seemed to comfort him. If he did die, his final hours would be eased. All of God's creatures deserved that much.

"Alright, then. Go get your blanket and pillow. You may sleep on the settle."

"Thank you, *Pappa!*" Stefan ran upstairs to retrieve his bedding.

"You are a good father, Nicolas." Sydney opened her dress for their fussing daughter.

Nicolas watched her put their hungry babe to her breast. "You have made me so."

Stefan reappeared and Sydney made room for her stepson on the settle. She patted his leg as he snuggled under his blanket. When Kirstie finished nursing, Nicolas turned down the oil lamps. The only light left in the room came from the fireplace.

"Will you be alright down here?" he asked.

Stefan nodded.

"Remember that Addie and John are just down the hall."

"I know." Stefan's eyes drooped.

Nicolas and Sydney kissed their son goodnight and went upstairs.

༒༒

The sun shone on a recreated landscape. Snow and drifts, some high as eight feet, blinded as they sparkled with the pristine purity that only an unspoiled snowfall can own. Bare tree branches glistened with their crystal coating.

Nicolas discovered Stefan on the drawing room floor, asleep beside the beast with his blanket tucked over them both. The dog had survived the night.

When the dog caught sight of Nicolas, he wiggled out from the blanket and lumbered to his feet. He stood with his head down, as if its weight was too much to hold. Ignoring the bandages on his paws, he padded forward in increments, his tail swinging back and forth like a slow metronome.

Nicolas knelt to pat his head and look into his eyes. "There's a good boy. Are you going to live then?" The dog licked his hand.

"He's alive, *Pappa*." Stefan stretched.

"He is indeed, son. I believe you sleeping with him helped in that."

Stefan nodded. "He likes me."

Nicolas did not want the dog to walk on his damaged pads, so he scooped him up and carried him to the kitchen. Addie fixed up a bowl of oatmeal and raw eggs and he gulped it down. Then Nicolas took him out to the porch to relieve himself and carried him back to the drawing room.

Stefan was happily allowed to eat his breakfast in there.

"Such a fuss over a beast!" Addie clucked, smiling.

Nicolas and Stefan were in the drawing room when Sydney came down with Kirstie. Nicolas laid Kirstie in a basket with a shiny bauble tied to the handle. She kicked and waved as she concentrated her gaze on the pretty thing. The dog turned to look at the new human. He struggled to his feet and plodded to the basket. Sydney jumped to her feet.

"No!" she yelped and pushed past Nicolas to rescue her daughter. Nicolas grabbed her arm and stopped her.

The beast turned to look at Sydney with soulful eyes and moved his tail in a long, slow wave. His huge head lowered to the baby's and he sniffed her hair. His tongue flicked out, and he sniffed again. Then he circled and dropped to the floor next to the basket, curled with his back to it, and sighed deeply.

"I believe we know his name, now," Nicolas announced. "*Beskytter* is Norse for 'guardian' so I believe we should call him Beskytt."

"I like that *Pappa!*" Stefan enthused. "Here, Beskytt! Come here, boy!" The dog lifted his head and wagged his tail. But he looked over his shoulder at Kirstie and stayed put.

"His feet still hurt, Stefan," Sydney reminded him. "He will love you if you bring him treats and pet him while he is recuperating."

Stefan slid close and stroked Beskytt's ears.

"When he is better, perchance he can walk you to school," Nicolas suggested.

"You hear that Beskytt? You're gonna take me to school!"

Beskytt wagged his tail and sighed again. His eyes closed and he basked in the loving attention of his new boy.

༺༻

Read more about Nicolas and Sydney Hansen at www.KrisTualla.com

Biography: Kris Tualla is pursuing her dream of becoming a multi-published author of historical fiction. She started in 2006 with nothing but a nugget of a character in mind and absolutely no idea where to go from there. She has created a dynasty - The Hansen Series - with six novels currently in line for publication.

Norway is the new Scotland!

A Woman of Choice - September 2010
A Prince of Norway - November 2010
A Matter of Principle - January 2011
And *A Primer for Beginning Authors* - April 2010

All books are available in print and Kindle versions online.

IF YOU ONLY KNEW

By Andrew Means

Old Bill Thaxton was never much for socials
And the townsfolk wondered how he spent his time.
He was rarely seen in the valley where the big ranches lay
As far as anyone could tell he'd hardly got a dime

His only known companion was a crop eared bruiser
A mutt of unknown parentage who followed at his side
If you wanted to see old Bill glare, the method was a sure one
Say a word against that dog and you'd need a place to hide

He'd say my dog may not be handsome
And he doesn't have a groomer
Clothes aren't to his liking
And treats are but few
But he's a comfort in the twilight
When coyotes are a-howling
He's a better friend than people
If you only knew

The street was kinda empty the day that dog came wand'rin
Kids in a pick-up swerved just to see him tack
He lay by the store till they figured Bill was ailing
Someone found Bill's body; he was buried by his shack

That dog was getting boney by the time the catcher got him
He was living out of trash cans and the neighbors weren't amused
Seemed like his time was up after two days with the county
Adoption's not an option when a dog looks so abused

They said that dog sure ain't handsome
He's way past need of grooming
You could dress him up and feed him
But it wouldn't hide what's true
Homes are for the snapshot teasers
Cute tricks and Mommy pleasers,
This one's no chance of saving,
If he only knew

Old Bill would roll over if he knew the fate awaiting
The syringe by the cage door, dog watching every move
They know, said the catcher, but there's no use a-moaning
Life's not for the mongrel and there's nothing I can do

Dawn was a-breaking as he opened up that cage door
He said you're one of a dozen if that helps to ease your mind
This world is for the cute ones, there's a surplus population
At least you had a few years and a master who was kind

For though you sure ain't handsome
And you wouldn't know a groomer
I'll bet a chew stick was beyond you,
A bed of fleece you never knew
Still, your eyes are full of trust
Though you're coated now with dust
You have what surely matters
A heart beating true

The needle it was ready and the dog stood awaiting
When the door was flung open, a girl stood by their side
She said I'll not see Bill's companion end his life in this way
There's many a day I met them while on horses I ride

TALES & TAILS

Though you don't know it that dog is a hero
When Bill was snowed under it's the dog that broke through
He fought off a cougar when Bill was trapped camping
It's a medal not a needle, to give him his due.

For though he may not be handsome
I'll pay for a groomer
I'll buy him a bed
And all the treats he can chew
I'll give him comfort in his twilight
When coyotes are a-howling
He's a better friend than people
If you only knew

"Life is as dear to a mute creature as it is to man. Just as one wants happiness and fears pain, just as one wants to live and not die, so do other creatures." ~ His Holiness The Dalai Lama

ന്റെ

"Man is the only animal that laughs and weeps; for he is the only animal that is struck with the difference between what things are and what they ought to be." ~ William Hazlitt

THE CAT CARES

By Nancy Marshall

One night, I broke a toe and could not sleep. I went to the living room couch to prop up my foot without covers. The cat leapt soundlessly to my side and pressed against me for the full hour that it took before painkillers put me to sleep. I could feel, through her cat-nature, her message: "I'm here for you." She was there when I awoke. The Spirit allowed me to know her cat-love through her furry presence, pressed softly against my side.

Drawing courtesy of John Green

WHAT NEXT?

By James F. Weinsier

Today I'm turning one year old.
It seems like yesterday....
I opened my eyes to see my Mom
Staring at me *that way*.
So many things have happened
During this past long year,
From meeting my new family
To overcoming fear.
Then there was that milk....
It's not the same as Mom,
But now she's not around
To help—and keep me calm.
And what about newspaper
I poop on every day?
I sure do get attention
Until it's tossed away.
Toys, noise, and teething rings,
All to keep me busy.
And everyone must pick me up;
It's enough to make one dizzy.
Learning how to bark,
Finding all that's new—
How much more is out there
Between one and turning two?

HALLOWEEN BRINGS A DARK STRANGER

By Andrew Means

An impulse took me beyond one of my regular walking haunts. The morning sun illuminated a classic Arizonan desert landscape of cactus and mesas. Surely my home office could wait for me to drive a couple more miles and take in the views of the mountains east of Phoenix.

My four dogs – a bichon, two bichy poos and a geriatric Springer Spaniel – had completed their routine saunter along the concrete path at the scenic vista parking lot. Anticipation was sated. They were content to humor me.

A couple of miles further into the Superstition Mountain Wilderness Area, I pulled onto the shoulder eager to contemplate the distant Four Peaks range. Hitching up Ricky, the energy bunny of bichy poos, I clambered along a rocky promontory until we had a hawk's view of arroyos and hoodoos.

On a weekday, before sightseers are on the road, the clarity and silence are such that even a bird call resonates. So a muted woofing from my other bichy poo, Sparky, back in my SUV, caught my attention. I looked for a reason, a cyclist perhaps or a coyote, but saw nothing. Sparky has a hair trigger in any case, I concluded. He'd bark at his own stocky shadow.

When Ricky whimpered by my side, however, it was a different matter. Ricky never cries wolf. Sure enough, no sooner had Ricky's feathery tail begun to sway than a black shape bounded between the rocks towards us. All that registered with me at first were alert ears and an ample wag. Indeed, the wag was about all that could be called ample. From a seemingly large head, the body contracted into washboard ribs and a waist that might have been the envy of New York and Paris runways. How the back end stayed attached to the front was a marvel.

Despite its skeletal condition though, this was a dog that clearly knew its own mind. And thus, as we returned home, we found ourselves with a hitchhiker.

Closer examination once we reached home revealed the newcomer to be a female who'd had puppies and appeared to be mostly lab. Her 27 pounds were well under lab weight, but there was no telling what her optimum size was before she began living rough. Her age I judged to be two or three, based on the tartar on her teeth and speculation

With our own four canines to cope with, my human companion and I quickly decided that a permanent addition to our household was not on the cards. Sheila the Springer had been found in the desert a year beforehand, and predicting her lavatorial routine was a challenge in itself. Sparky, the bichy poo, had recovered from Valley Fever and an operation to replace a cruciate ligament. But he still had to be handled a little delicately, certainly with more consideration than a boisterous lab might be inclined to show.

The decision seemed clear, and so I began contacting local rescue groups. With foreclosures adding to the usual pressures on shelters, however, it seemed all that was forthcoming was encouragement. Foster homes were already overflowing. Hearing of foster parents who already had large packs to look after made me feel a little bashful about approaching them with my own extra burden.

I reconciled myself to the notion that I'd be looking after the exiled lab myself, at least for a few days. But the one thing I wouldn't do if I could help it was bond. It would be difficult enough fitting a new muzzle into our tightly knit circle. I would have to stay firm, look after her but always with the idea that she was a temporary addition.

To that end, we decided that she would remain "the nameless one." If we christened her, it would surely be a step nearer attachment. The other resolution was that she would live outside – autumn now sapping the desert heat – and sleep in the garage. Allowing her to become a house dog, I could see, would be another step towards permanency. Fortunately, she seemed unfamiliar with dog doors. In her eyes apparently, the rest of our brood simply disappeared into the wall once in a while. I was not about to enlighten her.

In retrospect I was ill prepared for the task of fostering a stray. Although our bichy poos had been homeless before we knew them, they had come to us through a shelter and seemed relatively unaffected by their experiences. We sometimes speculate about their pasts but of course we'll never know. A dog psychic told us once that Ricky harbored no grudges, and indeed his happy-go-lucky nature indicated just that. Sheila the

Springer, intercepted on another desert walk, has only three requirements – food, water and sufficient floor space to sleep.

The nameless one, on the other hand, was needier and had more pent-up energy than a candidate for extreme makeover. After devouring a couple of bowls of food, she set out to explore her new surroundings. Familiar as I was with small and elderly dogs, I was constantly underestimating the curiosity and capability of this new arrival.

Our house has a deck accessible by wooden steps. A gate prevents our dogs from going up there, but it was no barrier to nameless one. The patter of paws from above betrayed her ascent, first to the deck and from there on to the roof. No doubt it was an elementary climb after the hazards of granite outcrops and cholla thorns.

No less of an attraction was our goldfish pond. I think I can confidently say now, based on recent research, that goldfish are immune to heart attacks. Otherwise, that angular black muzzle and those golden brown eyes looming above them would surely have caused multiple seizures.

Nightfall was no relief. My initial plan was to confine her in one of those plastic traveling crates during designated sleep time. The crate was lent to me by my neighbor, and had already been mauled somewhat by a previous occupant. No problem for nameless one. She simply gnawed on an existing hole until she broke out. I was forced therefore to let her have the run of the garage.

In the morning – early in the morning, when her barks awakened me – I found that she had interpreted "run of the garage" slightly more liberally than I had intended. Paw prints on the roofs of our vehicles revealed her nocturnal wanderings. She had reached heights – or depths, depending on one's perspective – I had rashly considered beyond her. A chewed container indicated a sortie along my work counter, while a scattering of purloined cat kibble on the floor was evidence of a record-breaking assault on a shelf a good six feet off the ground. Then of course there were the inevitable puddles and piles to clean up.

Even as she summoned my attention to these activities, shortly before dawn, remorse was clearly not on her mind. Instead she showed her delight at seeing me again by flinging herself against my legs in what might pass in the lab world for a bear hug and then rolling over for a belly rub. Her separation anxiety, I realized, was chronic. And no wonder. Who would ever know what she had endured out there among the coyotes and cougars? It was a wonder she could sleep at all.

Over the next few days she began to calm down. She put on three pounds and looked more lab-like rather than the Halloween ghoul she had appeared to be on first meeting. At night, she took to her bed as if it was something familiar from a previous chapter in her life. The fish even felt marginally safer.

Still, the fact remained that she was a foster child. Local rescue groups were on notice that we really were anxious to put her up for adoption before we got too attached to her and her to us.

While we were waiting for a vacancy, it was suggested to me, perhaps we should get her scanned for a microchip. In view of the remote place where she was found, I thought it to be nothing more than a formality. Collarless dogs are often dumped at city perimeters. Apparently their erstwhile owners think they go off to live with the coyotes. Why should this situation be any different?

As the vet tech ran her scanner over nameless one's back, there was an instant bonanza. She was chipped. I was stunned. A phone call revealed she had a name, Mallory. It also revealed an owner's name and number, and the rescue group from which she had been adopted previously.

Two days later, the owner had not responded. But the rescue group would take her back and find another home for her.

As I drove Mallory into Phoenix, I couldn't help feeling that I was betraying her. Despite my resolution, we had bonded just in the week we had been together. She had won me over with her affection and intelligence and that stoic good humor that makes dogs such an uplifting, irreplaceable part of so many people's lives.

I can't begin to fully appreciate the emotions of those who provide foster homes on a regular basis. Each parting must be bitter sweet. The sorrow of losing a companion outweighed, hopefully, by the prospect of a fresh start.

As we said our goodbyes, I could only hope that Mallory would bear no grudges and that fortune would bring her the happy, caring home she so richly deserved.

Biography: A. L. Means grew up in Britain and has lived in the Phoenix area for 30 years. He has written in various forms since a tender age, and has spent much of his working life as a journalist. In 2007, he published a memoir about the childhood of the late Country-Western singer Marty Robbins, who lived in the Phoenix area in the years before World War II.

> "...he will be our friend for always and always and always." ~ Rudyard Kipling

> "I believe in animal rights, and high among them is the right to the gentle stroke of a human hand." ~ Robert Brault

> "I have developed a deep respect for animals. I consider them fellow living creatures with certain rights that should not be violated any more than those of humans." ~ Jimmy Stewart

> "I think dogs are the most amazing creatures; they give unconditional love. For me they are the role model for being alive." ~ Gilda Radner

MY CAT, LOVER OF PEOPLE

By Amy Isgro

My brothers and I grew up with cats. We loved cats. Our house was perfect for the cat, as there were no houses in back of us, but a national forest. So every night, the cat would go out to roam free, doing his business, and in the morning, when we called for him, he came running in for his breakfast. We had three cats in all, one at a time.

Our last cat was named after the famous Russian author, Dostoevsky, but we called him "Dusty" for short. He was so loving, and people-oriented. He also knew that Mom didn't like animals, so naturally he jumped on her, as she lay on her bed. Then he turned his rear to her face, and started purring, digging his claws into her legs. And I heard, "AMY!! GET THE CAT OFF OF ME!" I couldn't help but laugh.

One Christmas in particular stands out. Now every Christmas, Dave, Greg, and I always played Monopoly. This one year, Dusty decided to get in on the action. Dave was winning, had his houses and hotels on the board. However, for the first time, I was coming in a close second! Wow! That is when Dusty lazily approached the board, and then lay right on top of the game, sending all houses and hotels sprawling! I screamed, "Dusty!!" But Dave, who spoiled him, said, "DON'T HURT THE DUZZ WUZZ!!" (That was his nickname for Dusty.) But our game was ruined. Our Christmas was not ruined though. It was one of our best. Naturally, Dusty had his own stocking as well.

Biography: Amy was born in December 1950. She wanted to go on stage, but was discouraged by her mother and drama teacher. She also wanted to teach deaf children, but wasn't given good instructions. She became a Speech/Language Therapist and worked with children in the school systems. She enjoys working with children. She loves cats and has also come to love toy dogs as well. She now has a darling Shih-Tzu named Candy. She is married, but no children. She has been fighting cancer for 20 years.

MERRY

By Melanie Thomas

Who does she think she is? Always bossing me around! She's not the boss of me! Kathy thought as she swung around and ran to the far edge of the field. Away from all their long laughing faces. She could still hear their laughter; her large brown eyes welled with tears.

I hate this place. I wish I had never come here. Every morning it was the same. Vincent would let each of the horses and ponies out of their stalls and lay down their oats in a trough. Kathy would at most grab one mouthful before the other horses chased her away. They were bigger than Kathy, their teeth were bigger too. Not to mention their back hooves, several of which had left large bruises and caked mud on Kathy's golden rump.

Rachel was the meanest; it was she who led the attacks against Kathy. She could think of nothing she had done to Rachel to deserve this treatment. She was just a small Shetland pony; the rest of the horses were thoroughbreds, big horses. Race horses. Kathy didn't stand a chance against one of them, let alone all of them at once.

So she ran away, just as she had done each morning since she arrived a week ago. She ran across the field as far away from the stables as she could get. There in the little corner of the pasture, where the big willow tree wound its roots into the stream bed, Kathy made her new home. She remained there all day until Vincent returned and led her back to the stables.

It wasn't too bad here; she had fresh water from the stream, plenty of grass and lots of shade to rest under. But she was lonely. There was no one to talk to, no one to play with and no one to race with. She knew she couldn't go on like this; already, her golden hide had lost some of its luster. She must find a way to leave here. Anywhere would be better.

Kathy made up her mind. She would find a way to escape. She'd had enough!

She walked the perimeter of the sun bleached wood post and rail fence. It was too high for her to jump, although she was a great jumper, she was just too small. After all, the fence had been built to keep the larger horses inside.

She kept a wary eye on Rachel and the rest of the herd; ready to bolt back to her corner if they came after her. For now, at least, they seemed content to graze near the pond and had taken no notice of the small pony inching her way along the fence line.

The pasture was big, and the fence followed the stream for a while before turning east into the sun where it hugged the tall oaks and poplars that made up the forest. Squirrels darted into the field, but ran back under the fence before the lonely pony could get too close. Soon, big fluffy white flakes flurried around Kathy's head landing on her long eyelashes. Kathy lowered her head and pressed on, inspecting every inch of the fence.

Her coat grew heavy with the snow; she shook it off and began to consider returning to her willow tree when she spotted it. There, the top rail had come out of the post on one end. It lay diagonally across the lower part of the fence.

The break in the fence surprised her. She really hadn't expected to find a way out. Vincent's ranch seemed too well kept for a rail to be down like this. Now that she had found it, she wondered if she really could make it on her own out there. She had never been on her own. *Where would she go?*

The snow fell harder as the small pony pondered her escape. If she waited, she was sure, Vincent or one of his hands would soon repair the fence. Kathy shook the chilly blanket of snow off, backed away from the fence, lowered her head and ran. She ran fast, for although the fence was lower here, it still came past her knees and would be a big jump for her.

She sailed over the rail, barely clipping her rear hoof on the fence. She stopped and looked back at Vincent's ranch. She wouldn't miss this place. At a trot, she made her way through the forest, carefully picking out a path through the snow covered underbrush.

The woods seemed to go on forever, the tall bare trees surrounded her. The little pony wasn't sure how far she had traveled, but when the light grew dim, she knew she would need to rest for the night. *But where? Out here in the cold? What if there were wolves around?*

She kept a brisk trot, focusing all her thoughts on a plan for the coming night. There was no place in the forest that looked safe enough for her to rest. Soon there was only moonlight bathing the trees in silver.

"Whooo!" *What was that?* A cold shiver raced along her spine. She turned her head from side to side, seeing nothing, she kept on.

Finally, winking through the tree trunks, she saw the familiar yellow lights of a house.

"Whooo!"

The startled pony raced for the lights. Her ears lay flat against her head, her legs stretched and her hooves pounded the frozen ground. Suddenly, her hooves left the ground. She tumbled, falling on her shoulder, her legs tangled in a wire fence.

Kathy couldn't move, the wire bit into her legs. She lay panting and frightened. The small pony whinnied for help hoping someone would hear.

Soon she heard movement near her head. She stretched her neck, turned and her eyes locked onto the biggest dog she had ever seen. The dog barked. Kathy whinnied in fear and struggled to free her legs.

The dog ran back the way he had come, his loud barks growing fainter. Kathy lay her head down and cried. *That was too close!*

Soon the dog began barking again, his barks grew louder—he was coming back!

She heard voices, men were coming. Kathy was too tired to struggle. She waited until she could see them, then raised her head to greet them with a quiet whinny.

It was Vincent! Kathy was so relieved to see him.

"There you are girl," his quiet voice soothed her as he patted her neck. "I've been searching everywhere for you." While Vincent whispered to her and stroked her neck, the other men gently unwound the wire from her legs. Soon she was free, she struggled to her feet and Vincent slipped a leather halter over her head and led her home.

As they walked, Vincent spoke to her.

"I've known you weren't happy, girl."

Kathy nickered softly in response and nudged his shoulder as if to say *I'm happy now*.

"I've seen how the rest of the herd treats you. To tell the truth, I thought they would settle down by now and welcome you." Vincent shook his head in puzzlement. "I've never seen them act this way for this long before. I guess we'll have to go with plan B."

What's plan B? Kathy wondered, but she was too tired to give it much thought. They were not as far from home as she thought. Vincent had taken a path to the road and within an hour they were home again. Kathy slept soundly tucked safe inside her stall.

The next morning when Vincent came to turn them out to pasture, Rachel and the rest of the herd soon chased her to her willow tree before she grabbed more than a mouthful of oats. Again, Kathy stood under the tree near the bank of the stream alone and wondered about Vincent's plan B.

Soon, Vincent approached and snapped a lead line to her halter. He led her through the gate to the same great rumbling cave box that had brought her here. Kathy pulled, refusing to step onto the black ramp that led into the cave. Vincent coaxed; Kathy balked. Finally, Vincent grabbed hold of her tail, wrapped it around her rump and pulled her by both tail and lead strap up the ramp.

The gate clanged shut behind her, while Vincent snapped the lead to the hitch and ducked out the small door at the front of the trailer. Kathy, left alone in the dark cave whinnied loud. *Let me out! I won't run away again! Please let me out!*

Then the cave was moving, gravel crunched under its rubber tires and soon it was rumbling down the road. *Where is he taking me?* The frightened pony worried.

At last the cave rolled to a stop. The gate was lowered and Kathy was backed out of the trailer. Her feet on the firm ground again, she looked at her new surroundings. A small house, rested between two ancient oaks. Kathy stood still as Vincent placed a blanket and saddle on her back and hitched the girth. She let him slip the cold steel bit between her teeth and slide the bridle over her ears.

She shied away and tried to sidestep when he brought the big red ribbon over and tied it around her neck. Then he left her tied to the trailer as he knocked on the door of the little house.

When the door opened, he shouted, "Ho! Ho! Ho!"

A young girl ran out the door and up to Kathy, her blond hair in pig tails, streaming behind her. She slowed her steps as she grew closer. Kathy looked into her kind blue eyes and liked her at once. Then the girl held out her hand, the pony stretched her neck to see what was being offered. Her nose caught the sweet scent of sugar.

Kathy's soft lips plucked two sugar cubes from the girl's hand. The girl stroked Kathy's head. "Merry Christmas, Sarah!" came a shout from the little porch on the front of the house.

"She's for me?" Sarah squealed in delight.

At the round of nods, Sarah threw her arms around Kathy's neck and hugged her. Kathy nuzzled her hair sniffing for more sugar cubes. "I'll call her Merry!" Sarah announced and kissed her forehead. Kathy was very happy with plan B.

Merry Christmas! She whinnied.

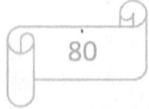

Biography: Melanie Thomas is a pen name for a local author that requests to remain anonymous for this publication.

"And God took a handful of southernly wind, blew His breath over it and created the horse." ~ Bedouin Legend

"Horse sense is the thing a horse has which keeps it from betting on people." ~ W. C. Fields

HOW TO GIVE A PILL TO A CAT

Author Unknown

Pick up cat and cradle it in the crook of your left arm as if holding a baby. Position right forefinger and thumb on either side of cat's mouth and gently apply pressure to cheeks while holding pill in right hand. As cat opens mouth, pop pill into mouth. Allow cat to close mouth and swallow.

Retrieve pill from floor and cat from behind sofa. Cradle cat in left arm and repeat process.

Retrieve cat from bedroom, and throw soggy pill away.

Take new pill from foil wrap, cradle cat in left arm, holding rear paws tightly with left hand. Force jaws open and push pill to back of mouth with right forefinger. Hold mouth shut for a count of ten.

Retrieve pill from goldfish bowl and cat from top of wardrobe. Call spouse from garden.

Kneel on floor with cat wedged firmly between knees, hold front and rear paws. Ignore low growls emitted by cat. Get spouse to hold head firmly with one hand while forcing wooden ruler into mouth. Drop pill down ruler and rub cat's throat vigorously.

Retrieve cat from curtain railing, get another pill from foil wrap. Make note to buy new ruler and repair curtains. Carefully sweep shattered figurines and vases from hearth and set to one side for gluing later.

Wrap cat in large towel and get spouse to lie on cat with head just visible from below armpit. Put pill in end of drinking straw, force mouth open with pencil and blow down drinking straw.

Check label to make sure pill not harmful to humans, drink a beer to take taste away. Apply Band-Aid to spouse's forearm and remove blood from carpet with cold water and soap.

Retrieve cat from neighbor's shed. Get another pill. Open another beer. Place cat in cupboard, and close door on to neck, to leave head showing. Force mouth open with dessert spoon. Flick pill down throat with elastic band.

Fetch screwdriver from garage and put cupboard door back on hinges. Drink beer. Fetch bottle of scotch. Pour shot, drink. Apply cold compress to cheek and check records for date of last tetanus shot. Apply whiskey compress to cheek to disinfect. Toss back another shot. Throw T-shirt away and fetch new one from bedroom.

Call fire department to retrieve the damn cat from across the road. Apologize to neighbor who crashed into fence while swerving to avoid cat. Take last pill from foil wrap.

Tie the little ***tard's front paws to rear paws with garden twine and bind tightly to leg of dining table, find heavy-duty pruning gloves from shed. Push pill into mouth followed by large piece of filet steak. Be rough about it. Hold head vertically and pour 2 pints of water down throat to wash pill down.

Consume remainder of scotch. Get spouse to drive you to the emergency room, sit quietly while doctor stitches fingers and forearm and removes pill remnants from right eye. Call furniture shop on way home to order new table.

Arrange for SPCA to collect mutant cat from hell and call local pet shop to see if they have any hamsters.

HOW TO GIVE A PILL TO A DOG

Wrap it in bacon.
Toss it in the air.

"Thousands of years ago, cats were worshipped as gods. Cats have never forgotten this." ~ Anonymous

---

"Dogs come when they're called; cats take a message and get back to you later." ~ Mary Bly

---

"The little furry buggers are just deep, deep wells you throw all your emotions into." ~ Bruce Schimmel

FRUITCAKE SUDOKU

By Penni Ferry

U			A					C
	E		R	C		K		
	I	T					E	A
T	C							
F	R	U	I	T	C	A	K	E
							U	T
I	U				A	F	C	
		C		R	K		A	
R					I			K

Solution is at back of book

PUNCHBOWL SUDOKU

By Penni Ferry

O	C		U	B		P		W
B			N	L	W			
						U	L	B
C		O		P				
P	U	N	C	H	B	O	W	L
W	L	H						C
H		B			P	W		
L							B	
				N	C		O	H

Solution is at back of book

SNOWFLAKE SUDOKU

By Penni Ferry

K		L		N		S		W
N								F
		F	L		K	O		
	K		S		O		N	
S	N	O	W	F	L	A	K	E
	A		N		E		S	
		S	O		F	N		
O								A
E		K		W		L		S

Solution is at back of book

NAMES FOR SANTA CLAUS WORD SEARCH

By Penni Ferry

Cross out the letters of the **CAPITALIZED** clue words as you find the words in the puzzle. The letters remaining that are not crossed out reveal a secret message from Santa. Some words appear separately in the puzzle.

CLUE WORDS (Remember only the **CAPITALIZED** words appear in the puzzle). The rest are for information only. ENJOY!!!

SECRET MESSAGE: _ _   _ _   _ _!!!

TALES & TAILS

H	A	K	A	N	A	K	A	L	O	K	A	D	G	O
N	D	E	O	L	R	N	B	P	A	W	H	E	A	A
E	E	C	D	E	A	A	O	O	N	I	N	D	G	N
R	L	I	A	O	T	M	Z	G	A	N	E	S	H	A
O	O	Z	I	N	S	T	I	R	M	T	M	H	A	F
A	C	O	D	A	L	S	C	E	A	E	E	A	N	E
L	S	B	K	P	A	R	B	Y	G	R	S	G	T	B
N	U	L	R	A	T	E	A	E	O	G	I	I	Z	N
A	S	E	I	P	A	K	T	S	S	R	W	O	O	N
D	E	K	S	A	N	T	A	C	L	A	U	S	R	A
G	J	C	K	N	I	N	M	Y	L	N	R	N	O	M
N	O	I	R	O	A	A	O	T	E	D	A	I	M	S
E	N	N	I	P	P	M	S	N	O	F	U	K	A	T
H	I	Z	N	A	H	O	T	A	N	A	K	O	K	H
S	N	L	G	L	L	N	S	S	E	T	L	L	H	C
A	L	E	L	E	E	O	O	A	R	H	A	A	S	A
L	E	P	E	T	I	T	R	B	E	E	S	O	U	N
U	N	A	M	H	S	A	F	A	P	R	K	S	D	H
K	K	O	L	Y	A	D	A	B	A	B	A	E	E	I
I	T	N	E	R	O	A	L	E	H	C	N	U	D	E
M	O	S	C	R	A	C	I	U	M	L	E	O	N	W

Aghios Vassilis
-Greece

ASH MAN
-Germany

BABA
-India

Baba Christmas
-Urdu

Babbo Natale
-Italy

BEFANA
-Italy

Bellsnickle
-Old American

Black Pete
-Belgium/Netherlands

Black Peter
-Morocco

BOZIC BATA
-Serbo-Croation

Bozicnjak
-Croatia

BOZICEK
-Slovenia

Christkind
-Belgium/Netherlands/
Germany/Switzerland

Christkindle
-Germany/Austria

DE KERSTMAN
-Holland/Finland

DED Moroz
-Russia

Deda Mraz
-Yugoslavia

DEDUSHKA MOROZ
-Russia

DIADO COLEDA
-Bulgaria

DUN CHE LAO REN
-China

Dyed Moroz
-Russia

TALES & TAILS

EL NINO JESUS
-Spain/Costa Rica/Mexico/
Columbia

Father Christmas
-England/New Zealand

GAGHANT BABA
-Armenia

GANESHA
-India

Grandfather **FROST**
-Russia

Gwiazdor
-Poland

HAGIOS NIKOLAOS
-Greece

Hoteisho
-Japan

Jolasveinn
-Iceland

Joulupukki
-Finland

Jouluvana
- Estonia

Julemanden
-Denmark

Julenissen
-Norway

Julgubben
-Finland

Jultomten
-Sweden

Kaledu Senelis
-Lithuania

KANAKALOKA
-Hawaii

KERSTMAN
-Belgium/Netherlands

Knecht Ruprecht
-Germany

KOLYADA
-Russia

HOLIDAY ANTHOLOGY 2010

KRIS KRINGLE
-Australia/Canada/U.S.

LE PETIT
-France

LOS REYES MAGOS
-Spain

MIKULAS
-Hungary

MOS CRACIUM
-Romania

MOS Nicolae
-Romania

Nikolaus
-Austria/Germany

NOEL
-Belgium/Netherlands

Old **MAN** Christmas
-Finland

PA Norsk
-Norway

PAI NATAL
-Portugal

PAPA NOEL
-Spain/Peru/Uruguay

Papai Noel
-Brazil/Peru

PELZNICKEL
-Germany

PERE NOEL
-France/Canada

RAUKLAS
-Germany

Saint Nicholas
-Europe/Belgium/
Netherlands

Saint Nick
-Australia/Canada/U.S.

Saint Nikolaus
-Germany

San Nicolas
-Mexico

SANTA CLAUS
-Australia/Canada/U.S./
Ireland/El Salvador

TALES & TAILS

Santa Kurousu
-Japan

STAR MAN
-Japan

SANTY
-Ireland

SHENGDAN LAOREN
-China

Sint Nikolaas
-Holland

Sinter Klaas
-Holland

Sinterklas
-Indonesia

Sion Corn
-Wales

STAR MAN
-Poland

Svaty Miklas
-Czechoslovakia

Sveti Nickola
-Serbo-Croation

Swiety Mikolaj
-Poland

TEL-APO
-Hungary

Three Kings
- Spain/Puerto Rico

TOMTEN
-Sweden

Viejo Pascuero
-Chile

WEIHNACHTSMANN
-Austria/Germany

**WINTER
GRANDFATHER**
-Hungary

WISE MEN
-Poland

HOLIDAY TIPS

By Karen Cafarella

As fun as the holidays are, they can also create a lot of stress. It is never too soon to start organizing your holiday "chores."

Food

Start by making a complete list of ingredients you will need for each meal you are preparing. By having a list with you when you go to the grocery store, you will only purchase the items you need. This will save you time and money. We could all use that around the holidays!

Cards, etc.

When it is time to send your holiday cards, start writing them out a few months before. If you have not received a card from someone in the last two years, consider removing them from your list. If you see local friends and family, there is no need to send a card. A fun idea: Cut up your holiday cards in small squares to be used as gift tags for next year's gifts.

Pack away lights, ornaments and keepsakes according to rooms. Throw away any damaged items. Keep outside items and inside items in separate boxes. What comes out first each holiday season should be on top in the boxes.

Keep holiday sweaters, purses, jackets and towels with your boxes. You will always know where they are when the holidays arrive.

Gifts

It can be hard to decide what to get friends and family, as most of us buy what we want all year long. Instead of exchanging gifts, donate to a charity in someone's name. If you want to give a gift, make it a homemade one. Fill a jar with different beans for soup, enclose the recipe. Buy picture frames you can paint and decorate. Buy candles and decorate them with shells and beads. If you knit or crochet, make something small for a gift. Everyone loves to receive handmade gifts.

Biography: Karen currently lives and organizes in Phoenix, AZ. In addition to running her own organizing business, she speaks at women's groups. As a freelance writer she writers articles for various community papers on organizing and other subjects. This submission is an except taken from her book, *Genuinely Organized: A Simple Guide to a Clutter Free Life*.

FAVORITE RECIPES

The following pages contain recipes collected throughout the years which our contributors regard as some of their family's hand-me-down favorites.

SPANISH RICE (WITHOUT TOMATOES)

Penni Ferry
Phoenix, AZ

1 large chicken
8-9 cups of water
1 pkg dried onion soup mix or chicken bouillon cubes
adequate to flavor 8-9 cups of water
1 Tbsp oil or 2 pats of butter
4 cups rice
10-12 oz jar of green salad olives with pimento
Parsley flakes (to taste)
Oregano flakes (to taste)

Using a 4 quart saucepan, boil chicken in water with soup mix or bouillon cubes until done. Set aside to cool. Remove and debone chicken, reserving liquid. Tear chicken into chunks. Strain liquid and set aside.

Put oil or butter into 4 quart saucepan over medium heat. When liquefied, add the rice, and stir to coat the rice. Rice may brown slightly. Add the reserved liquid, chicken pieces, olives, parsley and oregano. Stir well. Bring mixture to a boil. Lower heat, cover and cook for 20 minutes, until water is absorbed and rice is done. Stir and serve.

"We can judge the heart of a man by his treatment of animals." ~ Immanual Kant

FETTUCCINI WITH TOMATOES AND FRESH BASIL

Salvatore Saja
Glendale, AZ

12 ½ oz fettuccini pasta
12 ½ oz tomatoes
½ bunch of basil
5 Tbsp of olive oil
Salt, if desired
Fresh ground pepper, if desired

Wash and dice the tomatoes into small pieces. Season tomatoes with salt and pepper. Chop basil leaves into small pieces.

Boil the fettuccini in salted water, with 2 Tbsp of olive oil until al dente, then drain reserving a large cupful of the cooking water.

Pour the hot pasta into a large bowl. Add tomatoes, olive oil, and basil and mix well. Use reserved water to moisten, if needed.

Season with plenty of pepper and serve.

Serves four.

"There's no need for a piece of sculpture in a home that has a cat." ~ Wesley Bates

---

TALES & TAILS

STEWED CHICKEN & DUMPLINGS

Amos Moses
Phoenix, AZ

3-4 lb stewing or roasting chicken, cut up
2 tsp salt

Dumplings
1 ½ cups all-purpose flour
3 tsp baking powder
1 tsp salt
¾ cup milk
1 tsp minced parsley (optional)

Wash chicken pieces and place them compactly in a stewing pot or kettle. Sprinkle them with salt. Barely cover with cold water. Cover the pot with a tight lid and heat to boiling. Reduce the heat to simmering and cook until chicken is tender, usually 2 to 3 hours. About fifteen minutes before the chicken is to be served, add the dumplings.

To make the dumplings, sift the flour, baking powder and salt together making sure that the ingredients are well distributed. Add the milk and stir until the dry ingredients are just dampened. Add parsley, if desired, and stir until well distributed.

To add the dumplings to the pot, remove the cover from the stewing chicken. Dip a teaspoon into the liquid, then into the dumpling batter and drop it onto the chicken. Drop all of the dumplings in quickly then replace the cover and gently boil for 12 minutes. Remove the dumplings and chicken to the serving platter. The remaining liquid should be thickened enough to be used as a gravy for the meal. Serves 5 to 6.

"I love cats because I enjoy my home; and little by little, they become its visible soul." ~ Jean Cocteau

---

"If having a soul means being able to feel love and loyalty and gratitude, then animals are better off than a lot of humans." ~ James Herriot

---

"To err is human, to forgive, canine." ~ Anonymous

"To err is human, to purr, feline." ~ Robert Byrne

"Nature teaches beasts to know their friends." ~ William Shakespeare

CALAMARI RISOTTO

Salvatore Saja
Glendale, AZ

12 oz Risotto (Arborio)
2 white onions, finely chopped
3 cloves of garlic, finely chopped
2 carrots, diced
8 ripe tomatoes, skinned, seeds removed and diced
9 oz small calamari, cleaned
Salt and pepper, if desired
5 Tbsp black olives, cut into stripes
Fresh basil leaves
6 oz white wine
16 oz fish stock
10 oz hot water
5 Tbsp olive oil
2 tsp butter

Heat olive oil in a pan. Fry onion and garlic until translucent then add carrots and sauté briefly.

Stir in the rice. When the rice has absorbed all of the liquid add white wine and heat until it has evaporated. Then add 1 Tbsp of fish stock, and simmer over a medium heat. Stir until it's almost absorbed. Keep adding the fish stock in increments until it is all used up, then add the water.

Stir tomatoes, calamari, and risotto until the rice is cooked. Remove the pan from the heat and season with salt and pepper, stir in the basil, olives and butter. Serve.

NORWEGIAN MEATBALLS

Kris Tualla
Phoenix, AZ

1 ¼ lb lean ground beef
¾ lb ground pork and veal combined
2 slices soft white bread without crusts
⅔ cup light cream
2 eggs, lightly beaten
1 small onion, grated
2 small cloves garlic, minced
1 Tbsp chopped parsley
1 tsp salt
¼ tsp pepper
¼ tsp nutmeg
¼ tsp allspice
2 Tbsp margarine
1 Tbsp vegetable oil
1 ½ quarts beef bouillon
¼ cup flour
1 cup water
Salt and pepper, to taste

Mix together the beef, pork and veal in a large bowl. In a separate bowl, soak bread in the cream for a few minutes, then add to meat mixture. Next, add eggs, onion, garlic, parsley, salt, pepper, nutmeg and allspice. Mix thoroughly using hands. Then shape into 1" balls. Refrigerate for 30 minutes. Heat margarine and oil in skillet. Fry meatballs until lightly browned. In a large kettle or Dutch oven, heat the beef bouillon. Drop browned meatballs into bouillon and simmer covered for 20 minutes. Mix flour and water together, add to broth and simmer 10 minutes longer. Season with salt and pepper to taste. Serves 8.

"The Cat. He walked by himself, and all places were alike to him." ~ Rudyard Kipling

☙

"Animals are such agreeable friends - they ask no questions, they pass no criticisms." ~ George Eliot

☙

"If a dog jumps in your lap, it is because he is fond of you; but if a cat does the same thing, it is because your lap is warmer." ~ Alfred North Whitehead

☙

"If you have men who will exclude any of God's creatures from the shelter of compassion and pity, you will have men who will deal likewise with their fellow men." ~ St. Francis of Assisi

KWANZAA BEANS AND RICE

Amos Moses
Phoenix, AZ

1 cup chopped green onions
1 cup chopped green pepper
1 cup chopped red pepper
2 cloves garlic, crushed
2 cups water
2 Tbsp olive oil
1 can chopped or stewed tomatoes
1 tsp vinegar, to taste
2 16 oz cans black beans
Dash of salt, to taste
Dash of hot pepper, to taste
½ tsp oregano
3 cups of cooked rice (hot)

Sauté the onions, peppers and garlic in olive oil until tender. Stir in the tomatoes. Add a little of the water, vinegar, beans and seasonings. Add remaining water, as needed. Simmer until heated through. Serve over rice. Makes 6 servings.

> "The difference between friends and pets is that friends we allow into our company, pets we allow into our solitude." ~ Robert Brault

CANDIED SWEET POTATOES

Amos Moses
Phoenix, AZ

2 lbs sweet potatoes
4 cups sugar
1 orange, cut up with skin on
1 lemon, cut up with skin on
1 stick butter
1 tsp cinnamon
½ tsp nutmeg

Peel the potatoes. Wash them and cut into desired serving size pieces. Place the potatoes into a pot of cold water and cover. Bring potatoes to a boil and boil slowly for 20 to 25 minutes. Pour off most of the water. Add sugar, orange and lemon pieces, butter, cinnamon and nutmeg. Cook uncovered over a low heat until the mixture creates a syrup and sweet potatoes and fruit are candied.

> "It often happens that a man is more humanely related to a cat or dog than to any human being." ~Henry David Thoreau

> "The kind man feeds his beast before sitting down to dinner." ~ Hebrew Proverb

KUUMBA CREATIVITY SALAD OF RED, BLACK AND GREEN

Amos Moses
Phoenix, AZ

Create a salad by mixing together seven different ingredients that are the Kwanzaa colors of red, black and green.

Some suggestions:

Red	Black	Green
Tomatoes	Olives	Lettuce
Radishes	Black beans	Cucumbers
Red peppers	Eggplant	Avocados
Red cabbage	Raisins	Green peppers
Red onions	Grapes	Green beans
Kidney beans	Dates	Peas
Pimentos	Prunes	Green olives
Apples	Black cherries	Celery
Strawberries		Spinach
Cherries		Broccoli
Watermelon		Zucchini
Grapes		Honeydew
Plums		Pears
Mangoes		Kiwi
Peaches		
Raspberries		

Suggested dressings are red vinegar and oil, cucumber and dill or the sweet fruit dressing provided.

SWEET FRUIT DRESSING

Amos Moses
Phoenix, AZ

1 cup strawberry yogurt
Dash of ginger
Dash of nutmeg
Dash of cinnamon
Juice of ½ lemon.

Mix all ingredients together and chill before serving.

"Aerodynamically, the bumble bee shouldn't be able
to fly, but the bumble bee doesn't know it so it goes
on flying anyway." ~ Mary Kay Ash

"The bee is more honored than other
animals, not because she labors, but because
she labors for others." ~ Saint John
Chrysostom

"It is much easier to show compassion to animals.
They are never wicked." ~ Haile Selassie

NORWEGIAN WISH COOKIES

Kris Tualla
Phoenix, AZ

3 ¼ cups all-purpose flour
1 tsp baking soda
1 tsp ground cinnamon
¾ tsp ground ginger
¼ tsp ground nutmeg
1 cup butter or margarine
1 ½ cups sugar
1 egg
2 Tbsp molasses
1 Tbsp water
½ tsp grated orange or lemon peel

Icing
2 cups confectioners' sugar
½ tsp vanilla
About 2 Tbsp light cream or milk (to make a piping consistency)

Stir together flour, baking soda, cinnamon, ginger and nutmeg. In a large mixer bowl beat the butter or margarine until softened. Add sugar and beat until fluffy. Add egg, molasses, water and peel; beat well. Gradually add flour mixture, beating until well mixed. Cover and chill about 2 hours or until easy to handle.

Roll dough out to ⅛ inch thickness. Cut with cookie cutters. Place on an ungreased cookie sheet. Bake at

TALES & TAILS

375° for about 8 minutes or until done. Remove cookies from pan and cool.

Makes about 100 cookies.

Decorate cookies by piping icing from decorating bag into lacy designs on cookies.

Tradition is that you place the cookie in the palm of your hand and make a wish. Press in the middle of the cookie with one finger from the other hand trying to break it into three pieces. Your wish will come true if you can eat the entire cookie without talking.

"One reason a dog can be such a comfort when you're feeling blue is that he doesn't try to find out why." ~ Author Unknown

---

"Animals are reliable, many full of love, true in their affections, predictable in their actions, grateful and loyal. Difficult standards for people to live up to." ~ Alfred A. Montapert

SUGAR COOKIES

Dr. Trish Dolasinski
Phoenix, AZ

½ cup shortening
½ tsp salt
½ tsp grated lemon rind
½ tsp nutmeg
1 cup sugar
2 eggs, unbeaten
2 cups sifted all-purpose flour
1 tsp baking powder
½ tsp baking soda
2 Tbsp milk
Sugar to sprinkle on top
Raisins (optional)
Split blanched almonds (optional)

Combine shortening, salt, lemon rind, nutmeg, sugar and eggs and beat until smooth. Sift flour with baking powder and baking soda, add to shortening mixture. Add milk and mix. Drop level tablespoons of dough on greased baking sheets. Flatten cookies by stamping with flat bottomed glass covered with damp cloth. Sprinkle with sugar. If desired, press nine seedless raisins or split blanched almonds into each cookie. Bake in moderately hot oven (375°) for 9 minutes.

Makes 3 ½ dozen cookies.

SANDBAKELSER COOKIES
SWEDISH "SAND TART"

Leeann Rosckowff
Phoenix, AZ

Single Batch	Double Batch
1 tsp vanilla	2 tsp
1 tsp almond extract	2 tsp
⅞ cup butter, softened	1 ¾ cups (1 cup minus 2 Tbsp)
¾ cup sugar	1 ½ cup
1 small egg white, unbeaten	2 small
1 ¾ cups SIFTED flour	3 ½ cups

Mix all ingredients together thoroughly. Chill dough.

Bake As Follows: Press dough into Sandbakelser Molds (or tiny fluted tart forms) to coat inside. Place on ungreased baking sheet. Bake at 350° (moderate oven) for 12 to 15 minutes or until very delicately browned. Allow to cool for 10 minutes. Then tap molds on table to loosen cookies and turn them out of molds.

Makes about 3 dozen cookies.

NOTE: If you do not have the tiny molds for these cookies, shape the dough into balls and flatten for an exceptional butter cookie.

BISCOTTI WINE STICKS

Dr. Trish Dolasinski
Phoenix, AZ

½ cup butter or shortening
1 cup sugar
3 eggs
3 cups flour
3 tsp baking powder
½ tsp salt
1 tsp anise flavoring
1 cup chopped almonds

Cream shortening with sugar thoroughly. Add eggs, one at a time and beat well. Sift flour, measure. Sift again with baking powder and salt. Add to creamed mixture. Stir in flavoring and nut meats. Turn mixture onto a lightly floured board and knead until smooth. Divide dough in half. Form into two rolls the length of the cookie sheet. and ½ inch in diameter. Bake in a moderate oven (350°) for 30 minutes, or until rolls are firm to the touch. While still warm, cut rolls crosswise into slices ¾ inch thick. Lay these cut side down on a cookie sheet and return to moderate oven and bake 10 minutes longer to toast and dry out. Makes 4 dozen.

Note: These are called wine sticks because the Italian tradition is to dunk them into wine before eating them.

EASY BROWNIE TREATS

Chris Giles
Maricopa, AZ

Refrigerated chocolate chip cookie dough, the recipe provided or your own recipe
Refrigerated brownie dough, the recipe provided or your own recipe
Creamy peanut butter
Chopped nuts (Optional)
Grated chocolate, (Optional)

Frosting (Optional)
Use prepared frosting mix, the recipe provided or your own recipe.

Butter a 9 X 13 baking dish. Roll out prepared chocolate chip cookie dough. Lay it in buttered baking dish. Spread globs of creamy peanut butter on top of the dough. Roll out prepared brownie mix. Layer it on top of the peanut butter. Bake at 350° until a toothpick comes out clean. If desired, frost brownies and decorate with additional nuts and grated chocolate.

"Each species is a masterpiece, a creation assembled with extreme care and genius." ~ Edward O. Wilson

CHOCOLATE CHIP COOKIES

Penni Ferry
Phoenix, AZ

2 ¼ cups all-purpose flour
1 tsp baking soda
1 tsp salt
1 cup (2 sticks, ½ pound) butter, softened
¾ cup granulated sugar
¾ cup packed brown sugar
1 tsp vanilla extract
2 eggs
2 cups (12 oz package) semi-sweet chocolate chips
1 cup nuts, chopped

Combine the flour, baking soda and salt in small bowl. Beat butter, granulated sugar, brown sugar and vanilla in large mixing bowl. Add eggs one at a time, beating well after each addition. Gradually beat in flour mixture. Stir in chocolate chips and nuts. Drop by rounded tablespoon onto ungreased baking sheets.

Bake in preheated 375° oven for 9 to 11 minutes or until golden brown. Let stand for 2 minutes. Remove to wire racks to cool completely.

BROWNIES

Penni Ferry
Phoenix, AZ

½ cup butter or margarine, melted
1 cup sugar
1 tsp vanilla extract
2 eggs
½ cup all-purpose flour
⅓ cup cocoa
¼ tsp baking powder
¼ teaspoon salt
½ cup chopped nuts (optional)

Heat oven to 350°. Grease 9-inch square baking pan. In large bowl blend butter, sugar and vanilla. Add eggs. Using a spoon, beat well. Combine flour, cocoa, baking powder and salt. Gradually add to egg mixture. Beat until well blended. Stir in nuts, if desired.

Bake 20 to 25 minutes or until brownies begin to pull away from sides of pan. Cool completely before cutting into squares.

> "In the beginning, God created man, but seeing him so feeble, He gave him the cat." ~ Warren Eckstein

CHOCOLATE BROWNIE FROSTING

Penni Ferry
Phoenix, AZ

3 Tbsp butter or margarine, softened
3 Tbsp cocoa
1 Tbsp light corn syrup or honey
½ tsp vanilla extract
1 cup confectioners' sugar
1 to 2 Tbsp milk

In small mixer bowl beat butter, cocoa, corn syrup and vanilla. Add confectioners' sugar and milk. Beat to spreading consistency.

> "There is nothing in which the birds differ more from man than the way in which they can build and yet leave a landscape as it was before." ~ Robert Lynd

> "The bird of paradise alights only upon the hand that does not grasp." ~ John Berry

SANDWICH COOKIE TREATS

Karen Barber
Phoenix, AZ

18 oz bag of sandwich cookies (like Oreos)
8 oz block of cream cheese (not whipped)
Chocolate chips, melted

Crush the cookies. Measure out 3 cups into a bowl. Add the cream cheese and mix thoroughly. Roll into balls. Melt the chocolate chips. Dip the cookie balls in the melted chocolate. Roll in the remaining cookie crumbs. Makes about 3 dozen small treats.

"There are two means of refuge from the miseries of life: music and cats." ~ Albert Schweitzer

---

"Cats are the connoisseurs of comfort." ~ James Herriot

"A black cat crossing your path signifies that the animal is going somewhere. " ~ Groucho Marx

MINI FRUIT CAKES

Karen Barber
Phoenix, AZ

1 pkg refrigerated sugar cookie dough
½ tsp cinnamon or spice of choice
Dried fruit of choice, cut up finely
Nuts of choice, cut up finely

Mix the dough with the spice, dried fruit and nuts. Roll into walnut-size balls. Place in mini cupcake cups and place in mini cupcake baking pan to allow mini cakes to keep their shape. Bake at 350° for 8 to 10 minutes.

"Even the woodpecker owes his success to the fact that uses his head and keeps pecking away until he finishes the job he starts." ~ Coleman Cox

"Eagles: When they walk, they stumble. They are not what one would call graceful. They were not designed to walk. They fly. And when they fly, oh, how they fly, so free, so graceful. They see from the sky what we never see." ~ Author Unknown

CHERRY CHOCOLATE BARS

Karen Barber
Phoenix, AZ

Devil's Food cake mix
Can of cherry pie filling
2 eggs, slightly beaten
1 tsp vanilla
Chocolate frosting

Mix eggs and dry cake mix. Add vanilla. Mix. Gently fold in the pie filling. Pour into a greased and floured or greased and sugared 9 X 13 pan. Bake at 350° for 30 to 35 minutes. Frost using favorite chocolate frosting.

> "You think dogs will not be in heaven? I tell you, they will be there long before any of us." ~ Robert Louis Stevenson

> "No heaven will not ever Heaven be;
> Unless my cats are there to welcome me." ~ Anonymous

NO BAKE COCOA HAYSTACKS

Penni Ferry
Phoenix, AZ

1 ½ cups sugar
½ cup butter or margarine
½ cup milk
½ cup cocoa
1 tsp vanilla
3 ½ cups quick-cooking rolled oats
1 cup flaked coconut
½ cup chopped nuts

In medium saucepan combine sugar, butter, milk and cocoa. Cook over medium heat, stirring constantly until mixture comes to a full boil. Remove from heat. Stir in remaining ingredients. Immediately drop by rounded teaspoonfuls onto wax paper. Cool completely. Store in cool, dry place.

Makes about 4 dozen cookies.

> "Did you ever walk into a room and forget why you walked in? I think that is how dogs spend their lives." ~ Sue Murphy

NORWEGIAN CARDAMOM COFFEECAKE

Kris Tualla
Phoenix, AZ

10 vanilla wafer cookies, crushed into crumbs
1 ¾ cups flour
1 tsp baking soda
1 cup sugar
1 stick (1/2 cup) unsalted butter
3 eggs
2 tsp ground cardamom
½ tsp ground cinnamon
⅔ cup sour cream
Confectioners' sugar

Heat oven to 350°. Grease a 9-inch tube or bundt pan with butter; dust with cookie crumbs. Set aside. Combine flour and baking soda in small bowl. Set aside.

Place sugar and butter in bowl of electric mixer; beat until light and fluffy, about 3 minutes. Add eggs, one at a time, beating after each addition, about 5 minutes total. Beat in cardamom and cinnamon. Add flour mixture; beat until just combined. Add sour cream; beat until smooth, about 1 minute. Pour batter into pan.

Bake until toothpick inserted in center of cake comes out clean, about 50 minutes. Let stand 5 minutes; turn out on a wire rack. Cool completely. Dust with confectioners' sugar. Serves 12.

MIXED NUT SANDIES

C. J. Ewing
Phoenix, AZ

1 cup butter, softened
⅔ cup sugar
1 tsp vanilla
1 ⅛ cups flour
1 tsp baking powder
Salted nuts, chopped very fine

Cream the butter and sugar together. Add the vanilla.
Add the flour, baking powder and chopped nuts. Mix.
Roll into 1" balls. Place on ungreased cookie sheet. Do
not flatten balls. Bake in 325° oven for 10 to 12
minutes.

> "The dog was created especially for children. He is
> the God of frolic." ~ Henry Ward Beecher

> "If I have any beliefs about immortality it is that
> certain dogs I know will go to heaven, and very very
> few people." ~ James Thurber

> "All animals are equal but some animals are
> more equal than others." ~ George Orwell

PEPPERMINT BARK

Chris Giles
Maricopa, AZ

White Chocolate
Peppermint Candy Canes

Crush candy canes until fairly fine mixture. Barely melt white chocolate squares in top of double boiler. Spread onto lightly greased or sprayed cookie sheet. Sprinkle crushed peppermint candy on top of chocolate. Press candy into melted chocolate. Chill. Break into pieces. Serve.

> "I've met many thinkers and many cats, but the wisdom of cats is infinitely superior." ~ Hippolyte

> "Love the animals: God has given them the rudiments of thought and joy untroubled." ~ Fyodor Dostoyevsky

> "A bird does not sing because it has an answer. It sings because it has a song." ~ Chinese Proverb

BUCKEYE BALLS

Alfred Neill
Metropolis, IL

3 cups crispy rice cereal
1 lb powdered sugar
1 stick butter
18 oz jar of peanut butter

Chocolate Coating
1 package almond bark
¼ lb paraffin

Mix all ingredients and roll into balls.

Place ingredients for chocolate coating into saucepan and melt over low heat. Dip balls into chocolate to coat but leave a small portion uncovered to create the buckeye effect.

"I care not for a man's religion whose dog and cat are not the better for it." ~ Abraham Lincoln

"I think I could turn and live with animals, they are so placid and self-contained, I stand and look at them long and long." ~ Walt Whitman

MILLION $ BALLS

Alfred Neill
Metropolis, IL

2 lbs powdered sugar
2 cups flaked coconut
2 cups chopped pecans
1 ½ tsp vanilla
2 sticks melted butter
1 can sweetened condensed milk

Chocolate Coating
1 package almond bark
¼ lb paraffin

Mix all ingredients together. Chill for 12 to 14 hours until totally cold. Roll into 1" balls.

Place ingredients for chocolate coating into saucepan and melt over low heat. Dip balls into chocolate to coat.

> "Cats don't like change without their consent." ~ Roger Caras

> "The cat will mew, and dog will have his day." ~ William Shakespeare

PEANUT BRITTLE

Alfred Neill
Metropolis, IL

2 cups sugar
1 cup water
1 cup corn syrup
Pinch of salt
2 cups peanuts
1-2 tsp baking soda

Line a cookie sheet with foil and butter it.

Mix the sugar, water, corn syrup and salt in a saucepan. Bring it to a boil to the hard ball stage (265-270° on candy thermometer). Add the peanuts and bring mixture to the hard crack stage (290-300° on candy thermometer). Add baking soda and mix well and fast until the color changes. Pour in a thin layer onto the buttered foil pan. Cool. Break into pieces.

To test the cooking stage without a candy thermometer, drop ½ teaspoon of the candy syrup into a cup of cold water, then remove the candy.

The Hard Ball Stage - Candy should have lost almost all plasticity and be firm enough to roll around on a plate.

The Hard Crack Stage - Candy will form brittle threads in the water and remain brittle when removed from the water.

HOMEMADE GRANOLA

Renee Neill
Metropolis, IL

5 cups Old Fashioned Oats (Not Quick Oats)
½ cup vegetable oil
½ cup honey
1 tsp cinnamon
1 tsp vanilla
½ cup sliced almonds (Optional)

Mix all ingredients and place in a crock pot set on low heat. Vent lid slightly. Cook for 4 hours or until mixture is golden brown, stirring occasionally.

Delicious hot or cold, plain or with milk as a cereal.

Dried fruit, chocolate chips or M&Ms may be added when cool for a special treat.

> "If we treated everyone we meet with the same affection we bestow upon our favorite cat, they, too, would purr." ~ Martin Delany

> "Cats always know whether people like or dislike them. They do not always care enough to do anything about it." ~ Winifred Carriere

EASY SWEET & SOUR SAUCE

Penni Ferry
Phoenix, AZ

Bottled Chili Sauce
Cranberry sauce (jellied or whole berry)

Mix equal parts of chili sauce with cranberry sauce over low heat until melted or follow crock pot directions below. Stir. Add your favorite meatballs (frozen or room temperature), cut up hot dogs or smoked links. Simmer until meats are warm in the center and ready to serve.

Note: To prepare in crock pot, heat the sauces on high until the mixture begins to bubble. Stir. Add the meat. Lower heat and simmer until the meats are warm in the center.

The preferred recipe is to use 2 bottles of chili sauce with one can each of jellied and whole berry cranberry sauce.

Grape jelly can be substituted for the cranberry sauce. Sweetness of the mixture depends on the proportion of jelly to the chili sauce.

> "Time spent with cats is never wasted."
> ~ Sigmund Freud

BANANA LOAF BREAD

Amos Moses
Phoenix, AZ

2 ripe bananas
¼ lb butter or margarine
½ cup sugar
Dash of vanilla
2 eggs, separated
1 Tbsp milk
2 cups sifted all-purpose flour
1 tsp baking soda
1 tsp salt
1 tsp baking powder

Mash the bananas. In a separate bowl, cream the butter and sugar until light. Add the vanilla. Beat the egg yolks in a separate bowl then add to the butter and sugar mixture. Stir in the bananas and milk. Sift the dry ingredients together and beat into the creamed mixture. In a separate bowl, beat the egg whites until stiff. Fold them into the batter. Pour the mixture into a greased bread pan. Bake at 350° for one hour.

"Man is the only animal for whom his own existence is a a problem which he has to solve." ~ Erich Fromm

JEWISH BRAIDED CHALLAH

Pati Aufenkamp
Ava, Mo

Challah is the bread traditionally served at the Jewish Sabbath. This tasty bread is good enough to eat every night. The braided loaf is attractive with a firm egg-rich texture that works well for dinner, sandwiches or French toast. It is typically braided with three, four or six strands of dough (symbolic of love).

Dough

2 tsp instant yeast
3 ½ cups unbleached all-purpose flour
¼ cup warm water
3 large eggs
¼ cup vegetable oil
¼ cup honey
1 ½ tsp table salt
Corn meal

Egg Wash

1 large egg
½ Tbsp water

Sesame seeds or poppy seeds (Optional)

Mix the instant yeast with the all-purpose flour. Add the warm water and stir. Let this mixture sit until it starts to puff up (usually about 15 to 20 minutes). Add the eggs, vegetable oil, honey and salt. Stir until the ingredients are combined.

Turn the dough out onto a work surface and knead for about 2 minutes, or until fairly smooth. Cover with a damp clean cloth and let rise for 1 ½ hours or until dough has doubled in bulk.

Break the dough into three equal pieces and roll into long strips. Arrange dough strips on the table and join them together at one end. Pinch the pieces together before you start braiding. Braid the strips as if you were braiding hair.

If the strips begin to stick and blend into one piece, sprinkle with flour or cornmeal to keep them separate.

Continue until there are no strands left. Wet the ends, seal them together and tuck them under.

Next, sprinkle a large baking sheet with corn meal and place the bread dough on top. Fill an oven-proof bowl with water. Set oven on "warm" and place the bread and water inside. Bake until the bread almost doubles in size. Approximately 1 hour.

Turn up heat to 350°.

Beat a large egg in a bowl with ½ Tbsp water. Remove pan from oven and, using a pastry brush, lightly brush the egg wash over the top of the bread. At this time sesame seeds or poppy seeds can be sprinkled on the top of the loaf or rolled on by applying seeds with a dampened finger, if desired. Return to oven and bake for about 35 minutes or until golden brown. The interior of the loaf should register 190° on an insta-read thermometer. Let cool on wire rack.

> "The best thing about animals is that they don't talk much." ~ Thornton Wilder

The Original Starfish Story found in *Star Thrower*, a collection of essays by the naturalist and writer
Loren Eiseley, 1978
"One day a man was walking along the beach when he noticed a boy picking something up and gently throwing it into the ocean.

Approaching the boy, he asked, 'What are you doing?'

The youth replied, 'Throwing starfish back into the ocean. The surf is up and the tide is going out. If I don't throw them back, they'll die.'

'Son,' the man said, 'don't you realize there are miles and miles of beach and hundreds of starfish? You can't make a difference!'

After listening politely, the boy bent down, picked up another starfish, and threw it back into the surf. Then, smiling at the man, he said…'I made a difference for that one.'"

PET RECIPES

The following pages contain recipes collected throughout the years as special treats for our domestic pets as well as for wild critters.

BACON FLAVORED DOG BISCUITS

5 cups whole wheat flour
2 eggs
10 Tbsp vegetable oil or bacon drippings
1 tsp onion or garlic powder
1 Tbsp salt
½ cup cold water

Mix all ingredients together well. Pinch off a piece of the dough and roll it into a log shape. Cut into two inch pieces. Place on greased cookie sheet. Bake at 350° for 35 to 40 minutes. Let cool and store in airtight container. Makes about 40 pieces.

DOGGIE ICE CREAM

1 ripe banana
2-3 oz plain yogurt (Can be non-fat for dogs on a diet)
2 oz water

Mix all ingredients in a blender or food processor until smooth. Pour into small freezer-safe cups and freeze until solid.

> "Did you ever notice when you blow in a dog's face he gets mad at you? But when you take him in a car he sticks his head out the window." ~ Steve Bluestone

DOGGIE SOFT COOKIES

2 cups cooked oatmeal
½ cup raisins
1 egg
1 Tbsp maple or brown rice syrup
2 Tbsp apple sauce
2 Tbsp olive, sesame or flax seed oil
2 Tbsp whole wheat flour

Combine all ingredients in a mixing bowl. Spray or oil a cookie sheet. Using a tablespoon, drop batter onto cookie sheet in desired size. Bake at 375° for 20 minutes. Remove cookie sheet from oven, turn over each cookie and press with a spatula to flatten. Bake for an additional 20 minutes.

DOGGIE BONES

2 cups wheat flour
2 cups cornmeal
1 cup parmesan cheese
1 cup broth or water

Mix all ingredients in a large bowl. Roll out to ½ inch thick and cut with bone shaped or other cookie cutter. Place on cookie sheet and bake at 300° for 45 minutes. Cool in oven.

SAVORY DOG SNACKS

2 cups whole wheat flour
1 egg
½ cup non-fat dry milk
½ cup low fat or non-fat, low sodium broth (chicken or beef) from a can or bouillon granules reconstituted with water
2 tsp garlic powder
⅓ cup low sodium bouillon granules (same flavor as above)
½ cup low fat margarine
1 Tbsp brown sugar (optional)
2 Tbsp Parmesan cheese

Mix all ingredients together. Use additional flour or broth to adjust consistency. Roll out dough and cut into cookie shapes or refrigerate up to 24 hours and roll out later.

Bake on ungreased cookie sheet at 375° for 30 to 45 minutes depending on thickness of dough. Snacks should be lightly browned on the bottom and somewhat firm when done. These snacks will not be as hard as commercially prepared snacks.

৩৪৫

> "Old age means realizing you will never own all the dogs you wanted to." ~ Joe Gores

DOGGIE BISCUITS

2 ½ cups whole wheat flour
½ cup wheat germ
½ cup powdered dry milk
½ tsp salt
½ tsp garlic powder
1 tsp brown sugar
8 Tbsp meat or bacon drippings or butter
1 egg well beaten
2 Tbsp beef broth
½ cup ice water
Grated cheese (optional)

Combine flour, wheat germ, dry milk, salt, garlic powder and sugar. Cut in meat or bacon drippings or butter until mixed. Add beaten egg and broth. Add grated cheese, if desired. Add water as needed to form mixture into a ball. Roll out dough to ½ inch thickness on wax paper. Cut with cookie cutter. Cover cookie sheet with foil and oil it. Place biscuits on cookie sheet and bake at 350° for 25 to 30 minutes or until brown at the edges.

> "Until one has loved an animal, a part of one's soul remains unawakened." ~ Anatole France

> "A dog is the only thing on earth that will love you more than you love yourself." ~ Josh Billings

DOGGIE RYE CRISPS

1 cup soy rye flour
¼ cup soy bean flour
4 Tbsp vegetable oil
1 tsp brewers yeast (optional)
1 bouillon cube (chicken or beef)
⅓ cup boiling water

Dissolve bouillon cube in boiling water. Add oil to water. Mix flours and add to liquids. Mix well. Roll out to ½ inch thickness. Cut with cookie cutter. Place on ungreased cookie sheet. Bake at 350° until golden brown, turning once during baking process.

PUPPY FREEZER POPS

3 cups dry dog food
¼ cup peanut butter
¼ cup shredded cheese
1 Tbsp flax seed

Mix all ingredients together, coating the dry food with the peanut butter. Spoon into small (⅓ cup) plastic containers with lids, filling about ⅔ full then top off with water. Put lids on and freeze. Makes about 12 containers which is perfect for Border Collies. Make larger or smaller portions based on the size of your dog.

DOG BISCUITS

½ cup cornmeal
1 ¾ cups whole wheat flour
2 Tbsp garlic powder
2 Tbsp instant beef stock mix
2 Tbsp bacon bits
6 Tbsp oil
⅔ cup water
Meat drippings or bacon fat for basting

Mix all ingredients together. Roll out approximately ¼ inch thick and cut out with cookie cutters. Bake at 350° for 35 to 45 minutes, occasionally basting with meat drippings or bacon fat.

"Don't accept your dog's admiration as conclusive evidence that you are wonderful." ~ Ann Landers

---

"All of the animals except for man know that the principle business of life is to enjoy it." ~ Samuel Butler

---

"A dog wags its tail with its heart." ~ Martin Buxbaum

139

DOGGIE STEW

1 lb hamburger or ground turkey
6 large potatoes
1 cup macaroni
1 pound dry rice
1 large can tomatoes
2 cans yellow beans with juice
2 cans green beans with juice
2 cans carrots with juice
2 cups water

Mix all ingredients together and stew on stove or in crock pot until done. This recipe makes approximately 10 quarts. When cooled, divide into pint containers and freeze until needed. A pint serves an average 20 pound dog.

> "Lots of people talk to animals ... Not very many listen, though ... That's the problem." ~ Benjamin Hoff

> "You can say any foolish thing to a dog, and the dog will give you a look that says, 'My God, you're right! I never would've thought of that!'" ~ Dave Barry

> "A dog has lots of friends because he wags his tail and not his tongue." ~ Anonymous

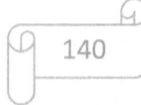

DOGGIE BACON TREATS

2 ½ cups whole wheat flour
½ cup wheat germ
½ cup dry powdered milk
½ tsp garlic powder
5 Tbsp bacon drippings
1 egg
2 Tbsp brown sugar
½ cup chicken broth
½ cup ice water
½ lb crisp bacon

Cook bacon until crisp and crumble it when cool. Reserve bacon drippings for recipe. Mix all ingredients thoroughly. Roll out on board to ⅛ inch thickness and cut into desired shape. Bake at 350° for 20 to 25 minutes. Makes 8 dozen. Store in refrigerator in sealed plastic container.

"The greatest pleasure of a dog is that you may make a fool of yourself with him and not only will he not scold you, but he will make a fool of himself, too." ~ Samuel Butler

---

"Animals are such agreeable friends - they ask no questions, they pass no criticisms." ~ George Eliot

DOGGIE BEGGIN' BISCUITS

2 ½ cups whole wheat flour
2 ½ cups bran
6 Tbsp protein powder (Soy or any flavor)
1 Tbsp brown sugar
6 Tbsp shortening
1 Tbsp vanilla extract
1 tsp cinnamon
1 egg
Milk to moisten (About ½ cup)

Preheat oven to 400°. Spray large cookie sheet with no-stick spray or cover with foil.

Combine all dry ingredients. Cut in shortening with pastry cutter or forks until mixture is the texture of meal. Add the egg and vanilla and mix well. Gradually add the milk and work the mixture until it can form a firm dough ball. Lightly flour board. Place dough on board and roll out to ⅜ inch thickness. Cut into shapes using cookie cutter or bake as a whole sheet and cut into squares when cooled. Bake for 30 minutes, or until biscuits are a little brown around the edges and firm to the touch.

> "I like pigs. Dogs look up to us. Cats look down on us. Pigs treat us as equals." ~ Winston Churchill

> "The average dog is a nicer person than the average person." ~ Andrew A. Rooney

TALES & TAILS

WILD BIRD PINECONE TREAT

Pine cones that have not been sprayed or preserved
Peanut butter
Wild bird seed

Smear peanut butter all over the pinecone. Roll the pinecone in wild bird seed. Hang the treat in a tree for the birds to enjoy.

WILD BIRD POPCORN & CRANBERRY TREAT

Popped popcorn
Cranberries
Kite string
Large eye needle

Thread popcorn and cranberries on kite string using a large eye needle to create a garland. A nice arrangement is to string 3 to 4 inches of popcorn and then string a cranberry or two. Hang it on the Christmas tree during the holiday season. Afterwards hang the garland outside in a tree for the birds to enjoy.

> "Cats have it all - admiration, an endless sleep, and company only when they want it." ~ Rod McKuen

PUZZLE SOLUTIONS

FRUITCAKE SUDOKU
SOLUTION

By Penni Ferry

U	K	R	A	I	E	T	F	C
A	E	F	R	C	T	K	I	U
C	I	T	U	K	F	R	E	A
T	C	E	K	A	U	I	R	F
F	R	U	I	T	C	A	K	E
K	A	I	E	F	R	C	U	T
I	U	K	T	E	A	F	C	R
E	T	C	F	R	K	U	A	I
R	F	A	C	U	I	E	T	K

TALES & TAILS

PUNCHBOWL SUDOKU
SOLUTION

By Penni Ferry

O	C	L	U	B	H	P	N	W
B	P	U	N	L	W	C	H	O
N	H	W	P	C	O	U	L	B
C	B	O	W	P	L	H	U	N
P	U	N	C	H	B	O	W	L
W	L	H	O	U	N	B	P	C
H	N	B	L	O	P	W	C	U
L	O	C	H	W	U	N	B	P
U	W	P	B	N	C	L	O	H

SNOWFLAKE SUDOKU
SOLUTION

By Penni Ferry

K	O	L	F	N	A	S	E	W
N	S	A	E	O	W	K	L	F
W	E	F	L	S	K	O	A	N
F	K	E	S	A	O	W	N	L
S	N	O	W	F	L	A	K	E
L	A	W	N	K	E	F	S	O
A	L	S	O	E	F	N	W	K
O	W	N	K	L	S	E	F	A
E	F	K	A	W	N	L	O	S

NAMES FOR SANTA CLAUS
WORD SEARCH
SOLUTION

By Penni Ferry

THE SECRET MESSAGE: HO HO HO!!!